to:
Louise K.

Best Wishes,

Marty Sweet

The Story of the Death of Hypatia

by

Marty Sweet

Bloomington, IN Milton Keynes, UK

 authorHOUSE®

AuthorHouse™
1663 Liberty Drive, Suite 200
Bloomington, IN 47403
www.authorhouse.com
Phone: 1-800-839-8640

AuthorHouse™ UK Ltd.
500 Avebury Boulevard
Central Milton Keynes, MK9 2BE
www.authorhouse.co.uk
Phone: 08001974150

First published by AuthorHouse 4/12/2007

ISBN: 978-1-4259-9190-6 (sc)

Library of Congress Control Number: 2007900345

*Printed in the United States of America
Bloomington, Indiana*

This book is printed on acid-free paper.

Author's Statement

Certain characters in this story were actual people, alive, and part of their times and ours as the past. Whether or not Mythological figures such as Prometheus, Zeus, Athena, Aphrodite, Minerva, Azeus, etc. were ever 'real' matters only in the mind of the reader, however, some would argue that myths must surely have had a beginning somewhere in reality. Nevertheless, Hypatia, Theon, Orestes, Cyril, and Plutarch were people who lived in the main time frame of this story. Other Biblical references to The Lord and His Disciples are personages based on accepted history. Some additional characters in this story are purely fictional and the product of the author's imagination, and any resemblance to actual people living or dead is coincidental.

Early Christian beliefs took different roads, not all imbued with the original moral, ethical, and religious practices as preached by Jesus and His Disciples. Even Peter and James (the brother of Jesus) had ecclesiastical disagreements as did Paul and the Corinthians. Recent discoveries shed new light on ancient sects of followers of Jesus, and their beliefs. The Gnostics, for example, incorporated several philosophical structures in their religious thinking, a fact that put them virtually at war with those of the Nicene creed, the Roman state-run Christianity. Deaths and persecutions over doctrines marred the blooming growth of Christianity. Many early documents of the Gnostics were banned, burned or otherwise destroyed, or hidden as historians and archeologists are now discovering. How much more is yet to be found, or has been lost can only be guessed at. Such is the nature of the dialogue of 'Hypatia.' Fiction is the filler and theory its companion. I hope my research into the story of Hypatia's death has proved accurate in as many facts as used to express her life and beliefs.

The Author

To understand the things that are at
our door is the best preparation for
understanding those that lie beyond

\- Hypatia

Author's Introduction

"And it was wonderful how in the lecture halls of Hypatia...the purest, most luminous wisdom in Alexandria was presented to the enraptured listeners. She drew to her feet not only the Pagans, but also Christians of deep and penetrating insight, such as Synesius. She was an influence of outstanding significance."*

"Sitting in the chair of Philosophy previously occupied by her father, Theon the mathematician, the immortal Hypatia was for many years the central figure in the Alexandrian School of Neo-Platonism. Famed alike for the depth of her learning and the charm of her person, beloved by the citizens of Alexandria...this noble woman stands out from the pages of history as the greatest of the pagan martyrs. A personal disciple of the magician Plutarch, and versed in the profundities of the Platonic School, Hypatia eclipsed in argument and public esteem every proponent of the Christian doctrines in Northern Egypt.

---

* Occult History - Historical Personalities in the light of Spiritual Science - by Rudolph Steiner (pgs. 20-22)*

"A number of writers have credited the teachings of Hypatia with being Christian in spirit; in fact she removed the veil of mystery in which the new cult had enshrouded itself, discoursing with such clarity upon its most involved principles that many newly converted to the Christian faith deserted it to become her disciples."*

"On a day in March in the year 415A.D., Hypatia fell victim to the fury of those who formed the entourage of the Patriarch of Alexandria."**

This short story has attempted to recreate the historical events leading up to her tragic murder. To do justice to her accomplishments is beyond the scope of my capabilities, especially in light of the scant number of documents that escaped destruction by the Christian monks and by the Arab General Amru. No known works of Hypatia survive to this day, though her accomplishments and contemporary praise of them is abundant.

The Age of Darkness stands as a testimony to knowledge lost by the inhumanities and injustices of man served upon mankind.

---

* IBID.
** The Secret Teachings of All Ages - by Manly P. Hall (pgs. CXVII -CXVIII).

Originally inspired by Carl Sagan's mention of Hypatia in his "Cosmos," and disgusted by Reverend Charles Kingsley's depiction of her in his book, "Hypatia: New Foes with an Old Face," written in 1852, this historical fiction is a tribute to a woman unequaled in the halls of beauty and knowledge, in compassion and dedication to truth, and devoted to these ends.

In Memory of Our Beloved Mother

Contents

Author's Statement

v

Author's Introduction

ix

Hypatia

1

Theon

19

Asclepe and Hypatia in Athens

39

The Delphic Oracle

61

Plutarch, Asclepe and Hypatia

67

Alexandria, Theon, and Pindarus

85

Orestes, governor of Egypt

95

The Lecture and Miracle
103

Cyril, the Patriarch of Alexandria.
113

The Murder
117

Theon, Pindarus, & Sufa Escape
125

Aftermath
135

Author's Apology & Sources
137

Hypatia

Hypatia stands at the center of her meditation room. Long, black hair hangs in silken strands from her tilted head. With gaze fixed upon a symbol - a Tau cross surmounted by an oval, shafts of golden sunlight lend a silent energy to her presence. Engraved in the alabaster molding below the room's high ceiling, the cross mesmerizes her. After soft chants and whispered invocations, a great teacher named Hypatia carries on an emotion filled soliloquy...

"How quickly cool Life's burning flames,
the fire shortly fades,
my father's dreams and my own aims
Cyril soon degrades...
O' murderous villain!
Behind the Cloth you hide,
from your pompous throne you seek to choke
the Life He gave when horribly He died!"

Asclepe, teacher, confidant, and good friend of Hypatia, waits for her to finish in a tall arched hallway just outside the room. Visibly disturbed by Hypatia's speech, she covers her face with shaking hands. Drawing deep breaths to steady herself, she enters the quiet room.

"Hypatia, the monks of Cyril demand your attendance in the Room of Questions, and will not be sent away. They are few, but I fear for your life. They are going to accuse you of some blaspheme, or try to trick you into saying something... I just know it!"

Hypatia was in a self-induced trance and the return to consciousness took several long seconds. Tilting her head back down brought sinuous waves to her soft, dark hair, now streaming down to her sleek waist and shimmering in the early morning sunlight. Hypatia's arms were back at her sides, her palms turned out and relaxed. Breathing returned to normal with three deep, even breaths as moments passed in silence.

Then, just as Asclepe began to regret her interruption, "Dear Asclepegeneia, Mother of Math, Sister of Numbers, it is only from ignorance the Nitrian monks of Cyril reek with fear and hatred. Amongst these few I would walk with the glow of your enlightenments and banish the pall from their souls.

"It was only moments ago, I felt a Presence as I spoke His Sacred Name, and now your being here gives movement to that impulse, returning to that Happiness again."

"Hypatia, how unlike you to speak of the irrational just so. On the one hand, they preach brotherly love, and then they run their Hebrew brothers from Alexandria with catcall and sanctioned banishment! A truly negative religion, I must say, and it is hard for me to understand why you find it so compelling."

"Compelling is a strong term. Frequently rewarding are my experiences with pure Christianity. Even Orestes shows the integrity of this faith in his dealings with the Roman citizens of Alexandria, the Jews, and other factions of our city. He is far more tolerant of the arts and knowledge than Cyril, yet dedicated to the tenants of Christianity as preached by the Apostle Thomas in his Gospel, as well as through 'The Traditions of Matthias,' by the Apostle of that name. Orestes and I have often spoken of Clement and his writings about these and other various original authors and proponents of Christianity."

Hypatia looked slightly up and away into another time as she spoke, "There is something very old hidden well within the folds of this religion. The threads of its origins stretch back to Apollo and beyond.

"I feel there is something, a Grand Theme perhaps, that reaches back before the Great Flood to a time of which we know so precious little. The Gnostics go too far, however, when they seek allegory with certain pagan myths."

Asclepe allowed only the briefest of moments to pass. Resolute in her intentions, and fearful of the monks' fanaticism, her response was quick and firm.

"The Christians are trying to destroy every knowledge we hold dear, my good friend. I'm afraid for you, Hypatia. The monks of Cyril are uneducated and are easily swayed to do the Patriarch's bidding. They are to kill you if they think you have blasphemed their newfound religion."

Hypatia was subdued, tranquil, making Asclepe aware of a change. The moment seemed suspended, or rather, blended with other speeds of time. The effect was mysterious and wonderful, but soon disappeared. As Asclepe caught the faintest smile slip from Hypatia's gentle face, she spoke.

"I can't help myself Asclepe. My father, beloved Theon, nurtured the rational, questioning aspect of my mind. I have no quarrel with the teachings of Jesus, the truth in His words is obvious and simple. Yet, I question the dogmatic beliefs some of His followers assume."

"It is for this reason I fear for you, Hypatia! You may be able to debate and reason safely amongst those of our way, you may even depend on the endless poor you have saved from disease and poverty; they call you 'The Nurse.' The well-to-do call you 'The Philosopher,' and love you no less. You are a balm and comfort for all Alexandria in these troubled times. Yet, Cyril would see you gone, if by death, then so much the more final. He has very little respect for Orestes as well.

"Again, Hypatia, come with me to live and stay in Athens. Cyril is a very real threat and has many eager converts to do his will, or worse yet to do their own."

Asclepe frowned, seeing she was getting nowhere, and spoke louder, "Hypatia! Our rational philosophy is scorned by Cyril! It brings truth to its students, and truth is far too dangerous for his monks to know. Has he not forbid them to attend your lectures except as spies? And we are better

5

off that it is so, though I know not why you bid them come at all."

Hypatia answered quickly, "There is a chance that many of them will see the freedom in our philosophies. They will be less entranced when Cyril preaches to them at his mass." She then spoke more calmly, with a confidence that she hoped would soothe Asclepe's fears. "Yesterday, a young monk approached me after evening lecture. He actually thanked me for my oration, and further told me that he now thought with heightened clarity of mind."

One last brief plea from Asclepe came weakly to her lips, "But, what of Cyril?"

"I never did like that one. His Christian acts consist of recruitment - more hands to carry out his conceited will. Those who will not follow him are discredited in the greatest glory of his Holy Father's Name. There are few like us that are truly safe from his prejudice and fanaticism. Orestes will protect us, so long as Rome rules Alexandria. Well, I shall meet with Cyril's monks now, and if nothing else, send them smartly on their way."

Asclepe thought to caution her once again, but before she could speak, Hypatia was away to the Room of Questions in another quarter of the Mouseion.

The peaked arch of the long hallway fell in sharp slopes to columned walls. Mosaics of fine detail and great beauty filled the spaces between the tall white ribbed columns. This was Hypatia's favorite walkway. Cool and dry, the hall had many busts of Ancient Greeks. Aristotle, Thales, Pythagoras, Socrates, and of course Plato, adorned the long Hall of Thinkers. Vertical ribbed half-columns were made of rubbed alabaster, polished to a glossy white. By contrast, the space between them cast many gray tones and shadows that were only highlighted by thin black lines delineating column from wall. Drawings of ornamental black railings created perspective and background. The aged bronze busts often caused unexpected goose-bumps when Hypatia accidentally caught a glimpse of their cold insightful gazes. Their staring eyes were housed in lifeless symbols of men long since gone, but the fire of what they stood for seemed to burn within them. Their empty gazes carried infinite meaning and memories. They were old friends, introduced by Theon when Hypatia was a child, and every bust brought a recollection of wonderful lessons taught through stories and tales. Too soon she reached her destination.

Massive doors gilded with ornately designed brass edges led to the Room of Questions. Hypatia walked to within ten feet of the doors as softly as a feather, but now the last few feet she made her stride known on the echoing marble floor. With resolute determination she almost flung one of the huge doors open, surprising herself as much as those within.

Hypatia knew she had to keep the advantage while a second's indecision gripped the zealous trio, and so, while yet in the threshold she quickly spoke,

"Aramachus Julio, and Petras, your souls look burdened for men newly baptized by the peaceful religion of Jesus." Hypatia suddenly realized the blunder of her cheerful honesty. Any derogatory comment, however mild, was a question of their faith and benefit in their belief in Christ. It would only provoke an irate response, but she spoke again attempting to avoid it.

"And, I wish to spend an afternoon learning from you of His great words and deeds."

The ploy had worked to a small degree, just enough to give her some time to reflect. While hoping she had neutralized their blind obedience to Cyril for the moment, she flashed back to the safe alternative of escape suggested by Asclepe.

And then Aramachus spoke, "We are relieved that you wish to learn of our Lord, we will gladly teach you. It was this burden you saw upon us. You would make a good ally helping us teach the word of God. We had hoped you wouldn't oppose us."

Julio nodded in agreement, but Petras added, "You must give up your pagan religions and lustful trysts with Orestes and others and follow the ways of our Lord!"

Hypatia easily endured the first insult; she knew the excitement of her mathematical and philosophical studies, and her knowledge of religions was far beyond their grasp. Newfound experience with the Christian Deity must have helped her suffer the further insults from Petras. Perhaps 'His' thought guided the words that followed. She spoke as melodically as a flute,

"To the highest peak of Caucasus,
in icy cold and frost,
bound with unbreakable fetters of bronze,
Prometheus lay upon *his* cross.
And every day his liver from his soul is torn,

while from the mountain sun
his heart pours out like water,
and the freezing winds
pierce his hands and feet."

Hypatia fell silent, her pause leaving them in a state of flux, suspended in time, waiting for her to continue; to re-verify her awesome command of oratory power. She did not disappoint them, but also brought them back to themselves,

"Lay no thistle thorns
upon the Ancients' graves-
It was they who nurtured Wisdom's seeds
with great and noble deeds.
Yet, only now their mindful maiden slaves
for their posterity and rhymes to save.
Oh Christian monks, bring your minds to view
the similarities of ancient lore and new:
Prometheus brought in fennel stalk
the fire of Zeus for men to share.
That man be warmed,
and see in darkest night,
a martyr's role he earned..."

Hypatia had manifested a somber mood, capturing the three with subtle verbal nuance and slowly, hypnotically, she continued,

"See you not the irony of what was once,
     now is, and what will be?
It's of you Jesus sings
     when the light to you He brings!"

The monks were appeased when they heard 'maiden,' and also an apparent kudo for their religious natures. Hypatia now had to contend, however, with complimented egos, not to mention some momentum the trio *still* had from their unrelenting religious fervor. Hypatia contemplated the veracity of the analogy of Prometheus and Jesus. The fact that she shared a pagan myth with their Lord escaped them, yet other words would have been better used. "Maybe something about the Apostles," she thought…"something about Paul's teachings."

The monks were no longer hostile, however, at least temporarily, and this gave Hypatia a moment's respite from their aggressively blind arrogance.

Aramachus, short and bulky, showed his Hebrew characteristics. Tightly curled black hair covered his head and face and dropped to a pointed beard ending just below his chest. His eyebrows hung thick and jet-black above passionate brown eyes. He wore a dark tunic trimmed with gray and white stripes on its seams and around his neckline, but no longer displayed his chest plate, sash, or other relics of previous beliefs. He began to speak, going so far as to raise a forefinger and open his mouth, but as quickly withdrew into reflection. Hypatia knew Aramachus would be the most dangerous of the three, but also the easiest to sway. He wore on his bearded face the wrinkled lines of inner doubt, a pain that spoiled the euphoria of his recent religious conversion.

Suddenly Petras spoke in a tone of imperious authority, simple and raw, "Woman, the great Apostle Paul warned us of the likes of you, for he said, '…unto the unmarried and the widows, it is good for them that they abide even as I. But if they cannot contain, let them marry: for it is better to marry than to burn.'

"And yet, Orestes and countless others parade in and out of your door at will, and we think you a harlot and worse yet, a tempter and advocate of false pagan beliefs. Why have you not married Orestes? We know he is of your kind and wishes this. Marry in the eyes of our Lord and lead the life of a true Christian. Denounce pagan religions, or did you take us for fools and think that with a few compliments you might tempt us away from our appointed tasks?

"You say we are as lights of our Lord's love- we know that! Are you truly ready for the light of our Lord? If so, purify yourself, condemn now all your false gods and doctrines. Clear the rubble of pagan teachings from your life and let us teach you the true path, and the part a woman of God must play!"

Hypatia withdrew deep into thought and deep into her spirit as a solid resolution gripped her and grew to the flexed contours of arms and fists at her sides. She stood motionless as the room quickly grew colder. Time and movement became suspended in the freezing vacuum of the room's space. Stars everywhere burst into appearance against the dark vastness of the void. They were between the earth and the moon- much nearer, it seemed, the ivory glow of a full moon than the blue and white earth falling away below them. The monks immediately felt the drop in temperature, and after endless seconds they could see their breathes. It became so cold, Julio stood nearer to Hypatia to be warmed by the eternal fire felt in her soul, enrapturing her spirit. Aramachus and Petras quickly followed suit and stood by Julio.

They did not know what they were standing on and were very afraid.

·······

After Hypatia brought them back, Aramachus was totally disarmed, all his hostilities were gone, and he even thanked Hypatia as they were leaving. Julio bowed and assured her that he would always be at her service should she need him. Petras was quiet, but also not happy by appearance, and this worried Hypatia. She was about to say something before he completely left the room, but at the door he turned.

"Farewell, good Hypatia. A voice calls to me from a far place, and I must heed it or face the wrath of Cyril. I don't know how or why I ever believed him…he is…"

"The trouble you had came from believing *Cyril's* words, and not the words of your Lord Savior. Follow Him."

"He seems closer to me now that my heart has been opened to Him, yet still He is as a stranger to me. My family and I will seek Him."

"Go in peace Petras, and remember, a stranger is a friend you have not become acquainted with yet. As you get to know Him, you will find He is a good and true friend."

Petras was gone, and the Room of Questions empty but for Hypatia. The strain she had sustained was only slightly relieved by a deep breath. As she slumped on a marble bench she smiled at its coldness. The difficulty with them had been more than expected. Without help, they would have been a frightening trio of men to deal with. Hypatia had underestimated the influence Cyril had on Petras, and knew he had misinterpreted Paul's words to use them for his own agenda. Hypatia contemplated that their Savior may have helped save her from them.

·······

Sufa, a young student of Hypatia's quietly enters the room. She is radiant with the wide-eyed energy of her youth. Her braided black hair shines like starlight. She stands silently for many minutes with firm Nubian arms at her sides waiting for Hypatia to look up and see her. Finally, she can hold her voice no longer, and whispers softly,

"Teacher, it is I, Sufa. May I speak with you?"

"Yes, Sufa. What is it?"

"The forty-seventh Proposition of Euclid, notable master of Mathematics, may I have an answer to my curiosity?"

"Yes Sufa. Go on."

"Are the relationships of these numbers symbolic, perhaps lost from some earlier age?"

"Yes, they are. And no, they are not completely lost, though you should know that the forty-seventh Proposition belongs to Pythagorus, though we are indebted to Euclid for ordering many of his works. The great Ionian Teacher was the world's first philosopher, named for the Pythian Oracle at Delphi that prophesied his birth."

Their conversation wound its way through the life of Pythagorus and eventually to the right triangle.

"According to Plutarch, Pythagorus established a relationship between the geometrical solids and the aspects of God. There are only five symmetrical geometric solids, of course." Sufa did not know, but politely noted this interesting information.

Hypatia continued, "Plutarch also states that Universal Nature is made up of three things: Intelligence, Matter, and a combination of both called Kosmos. Plato calls them: Idea, or Father; Mother, or place of Generation; and Offspring, or Production."

Hypatia stopped talking as a flood of ideas poured in on her reflecting mind, not the least of which was the Christian idea of the Trinity, first expounded upon in the Nicean Creed of 325.

"Go now and ponder these things Sufa, I must meet with Master Theon."

"Yes teacher. Thank you."

Hypatia smiled in answer, and returned to her contemplations.

Theon

Theon was a handsome man, young looking for his sixty-four years, and overshadowed in accomplishment only by his daughter, Hypatia. Neatly cropped silver-gray hair gave the impression of superior intellectual knowledge and authority, yet he was loved and respected for his humanity by all who knew him. His speech carried a robust tone and an even clarity, especially for his medium frame.

"Hypatia, there is no end to the courtings of Orestes. He uses his position and Roman authority to call upon you ceaselessly. And I feel he is gracious to us only because of infatuation with your beauty and knowledge. Are the gods truly dying, abandoning us to the Roman authorities as well as Cyril and the barbarians? We seem to be caught in some grand play, a struggle between religions and politics for power. There is no longer time for wisdom, knowledge, history, and the sciences. It is all about power. And how will you handle Orestes? You know he seeks your hand."

Hypatia suppressed a giggle as she spoke, "Would you call me Aphrodite, father? Or rename me Athena in honor of Zeus' own? I would rather you think of me as Minerva, the name you gave me yesterday after Orestes came to call."

"Ah, yes, I remember how you laughed when I said Minerva ruled your heart, and glad I am too! Yet, why Orestes encourages Cyril's monks to attend the Roman Theater to spy on the Jews is unknown to me. Maybe he is hinting that he could do the same with your lectures, suggesting to you by this act that you would be the more protected under the auspices of marriage to him. I don't like him or the way he pits one religion against the other. He helps the cause of war between the Jews and Cyril's Christians. Some of the Jews have already attacked certain Christians in their homes merely because of their presence as spies in the theater.

"I feel that it is more than we shall be able to endure, that the only true safety will be in escape. I am afraid of what is coming."

Hypatia frowned so seldom the act startled Theon.

"Life here is precious, father. If Orestes were to be insulted or turned from his attention toward me, it is conceivable that he would give us to the Nitrian monks. Yet, he professes Christianity as his religion, and in some ways is righteous in his devotion to its creeds."

"Cyril claims his devotions are lacking by his constant attention to you! He attends as many of your lectures as the office of Prefect allows, and this severely annoys Cyril. And I don't like the things the monks say of you and Orestes, the things they imply merely from his frequent visits."

"I don't care what they say!"

Hypatia spoke proudly, as her head tilted ever so slightly back and up to indicate that she meant what she said. She tried not to worry Theon any further, but added, "The monks should know that when Orestes asked me for my hand, I told him that I could not, for I am wed to Truth. This was as far as I could go. I dare not directly tell him no, nor slight his intentions. Yet, we discuss many things philosophical and intellectual, and his faith is peaceful compared to Cyril's fanaticism. He is tolerant towards others, *and*, his Roman authority will keep Cyril somewhat at bay as long as Rome yet survives the Goths. The Patriarch fears of all, the Goths most, and welcomes any allegiance against them. He worries much less about us than they. And, so far, they remain obedient to the Roman authorities. Our school is an annoyance to him, yet he treads slowly against us while Orestes graces us with his visits."

Theon was not comforted, and replied absently, "Yes, that is so, Hypatia." Theon spoke, but his mind was dwelling on the future and its promise, or lack of it. Then, in a hopeful tone, "We will leave soon. Yes, you must not disturb the sleeping lion. We must see that he sleeps soundly and does not awake with a desire to go with you to Athens. The man is unrelenting."

Hypatia was about to leave for a vacation, and did not wish to worry her father again, and so let the moments pass saying nothing. Before long, a young man walked in, bowed, and placed upon a low wood table a bowl of dates and other sweet fruits. The clay bowl was fired with blue lines and geometric figures on a white background. The student waited for a moment, then turned to leave.

"Wait Pindarus. Will you not join us?" Theon especially liked his student, and welcomed conversation.

"I would not wish to interrupt you and your daughter, Master Theon."

Hypatia also liked Pindarus' company, but now more for diversion than any altruistic dialogues.

She was not ungrateful, however, and only genuine interest toned a light reply.

"Please stay, Pindarus. Perhaps we will speak of astronomy if father allows us, though he would wish to speak with you of Pythagorus and his Geometry all day and night if we should let him!"

Pindarus was secretly amazed at Hypatia's perspicacity. The moment she had alluded to geometry, his gaze went from her silent green eyes to the bowl of fruits. At that instant, he relived the preparations of their snack and all the young hopes he had for their favor. He thought the Tau cross and geometric designs etched on the bowl would please Theon, perhaps evoke a short conversation, and now here he was sharing a meal with them both!

"Pindarus, how is your research treating you? As I understand it, Synesius gave you some information regarding the sayings of Thomas."

"During his last visit he gave us much to study…" He nodded slightly in Hypatia's direction and continued, "Thomas assumes the role of mystic philosopher in the sayings he attributes to Jesus. He writes that Jesus said, 'Whoever searches will find. It will be opened to him.' As I search for material

I find this is true. The Coptics use the Greek copy of His sayings, but there is an older composition from Jerusalem during the Roman war against the Jews. No one knows if it survived the fires and Roman desecrations of those years, but to read His words in Aramaic, from the source closest to His inspiration would be an experience."

"Many original truly great writings have been lost through the years." Hypatia reflected for a moment, then went on, "Matthias, the Apostle elected after the death of Jesus, also had a book. Clement wrote of it."

Theon held the chair in Philosophy in the Great Library, but he was mostly preoccupied with the Classics. He didn't think of Christians as philosophers before, but now more depth was being added to his understanding, and he was intrigued. Learning comes from discussion, and so the three talked of the works of various Christian Apostles for the rest of the afternoon.

....

Several hours later, Theon and his lovely daughter looked out from their large second story window to the city streets. Their home afforded a magnificent view of Alexandria, from the wide cobbled streets directly below to the wharves with sailing ships docked for load and unload a mile or more away. The recessed window framed their two figures like a portrait as they perused Alexandria from their vantage.

"Have you finished your research into the ancient Egyptian and Greek documents, Hypatia?"

Hypatia turned to her father and smiled with a blossoming radiance.

"Oh, father, noble teacher of Pythagorian truth, master of Euclidian order, most knowledgeable instructor of mathematics, I can answer either yes or no!"

Theon was filled with pride and happiness. He loved his daughter very much. Long ago when her mother had died, he sent word to his friend Plutarch in Athens. Plutarch responded by sending three women from different Mystery schools to instruct and help in playing the role of mother to Hypatia. As Hypatia grew, Theon came to virtually worship his daughter as Wisdom incarnate, and, as mentor, thrilled at the role *he* played in her life. Never forgetting the emotional side, Theon was always quick with a hug or a funny story to smooth away the pains of growing up. Hypatia's fame spread rapidly as she matured into a legend of perfect beauty and brilliant intellect. Many noblemen and aristocrats journeyed from far lands to seek her hand. Most became her pupils, though some who sought her in marriage merely returned from whence they came. When Theon realized in Hypatia's nineteenth year that she had surpassed him in knowledge as well as fame, he had experienced the happiest moment in his life. From that time on, Theon felt a sense of accomplishment very few others could only dream of.

It was total pride that filled him when he began to pace in a counterclockwise circle. With hands behind his back and gaze directed up and away, he stopped, then bent his head in contemplation and began pacing again.

When he stopped, he replied, "Well, yes, perhaps your honorifics are based somewhat in truth from your point of view, but, you see, by these declarations your circumlocutions prevent an accurate answer to my question."

Hypatia laughed, "Oh father, I love you so! Come with me to my study room at the library and I will show you what I have found."

"I love you too, my precious one, but this time let's leave the chariot here and walk. It's cooling now and our return will be in wondrous twilight."

Hypatia hopped down from the window sill and walked to Theon. They hugged for a few infinite seconds, then left for the Great Library of Alexandria.

It was a good time for walking. The wide cobblestone road afforded room for chariot and pedestrians alike. The streets were empty at this time of day as shopkeepers one by one withdrew merchandise from in front of their shops. As a fruit vendor began his evening tasks of closing, the pair approached.

"Good evening shopkeeper Selenus, I hope your day has been fruitful."

Hypatia and Selenus both groaned at Theon's pun.

"No offense master Theon, but today's sales are as empty of profit as your pun is of humor."

"No offense taken, dear sir, I'm sorry your business is not doing well."

"They've run some of the Jews off, and more each day. They were half of my business. The Jews are no less vicious in their attacks on Christians. Now, Cyril sends his monks about collecting 'donations' for the 'needy' to further lessen my profits. Between you and I, I'll wager it's Cyril's fat stomach that contains my delicious donated fruit. I wish Orestes would put more restraints on him."

The last remark contained a not-so-subtle implication directed at Hypatia. Without losing a heartbeat, she explained to him that they had no leverage over the dictates of either Orestes or Cyril, but that they would talk to the Prefect about it. Selenus was very happy, for he knew how much Orestes adored Hypatia, and that he would do all he could for her to the smallest detail. What he didn't realize was that Orestes was somewhat cold and calculating. He gave up favors grudgingly, and only if they somehow resulted in benefit to him. Selenus gave them each an apple as they exchanged parting words.

As they walked away Theon turned to his progeny, "Hypatia, I worry about these times. Why don't we join Plutarch in Athens? He has invited us in a letter to Asclepe, so she tells me."

"Did we not discuss this before, father? My work and life are here in Alexandria. Besides, rumor has it that I will soon receive a chair in Philosophy at the library."

"That is no rumor, dear one. I suggested my retirement to the chief librarians and they unanimously agreed that they would honor this change. Yet, I wish I hadn't, for I thought it would protect you. Now I fear that it may only serve to cause you center stage in Alexandria's struggle. Protection that is sure can only be in escape."

"No, father, truth and knowledge must never run away, for they can never be bound."

"I pray your convictions aren't influenced by naivety, my child."

"Father it disturbs me to hear you speak so. I mean no disrespect, but I am a full grown woman and my dedication is to the library, as is yours. Long years have been spent in learning, teaching, and lecturing. Alexandria yet contains the ancient knowledge of the world. We must preserve it for future generations. Theodosius tried to destroy all pagan temples, including the Serapeum part of the library by edict some years ago, remember? It was thought that most of the scrolls and manuscripts were destroyed by fire, but it was not so. The delicate papyri were removed prior to the fire and secreted in a librarian's home; Thelsius was his name. I have discovered these and brought them back to my study under the library lecture hall that

I use. What's more, through them I have learned that the most ancient or sacred works were stored in fireproof containers. Many documents were inscribed in clay and also survived. They have been hidden in the Mystery chambers beneath the Sphinx and the Great Pyramid, and in a sacred temple in India. Unfortunately, I have not yet discovered *exactly* where. I am sure they contain most of the secret knowledge lost before and just after the Great Flood, and the Gospels of Apostles that lived during the time of the Christian Lord and Savior, Ea-shoa' M'shee-kha, The Anointed Life-Giver. We must find and establish this knowledge for posterity.

"Now you see why I can't think of leaving Alexandria, father. Though I've learned much, now I've found that there is much more to learn, and know that my work has just begun."

Hypatia and Theon strolled leisurely past the closing shops, acknowledging greetings from many passers-by.

When it concerned his daughter, Theon was not sure that risking life was an appropriate action to take for the sake of truth, knowledge, wisdom, or any metaphysical endeavor. Yet, he would give *his* life instantly for her convictions. As they walked, his thought brought the realization that he was a victim of love for his child, and, first and foremost, concerned for her safety.

They walked down, around a sharp bend, and into the broad East courtyard, also cobbled, and approached the near edge of the Mouseion. The large rectangular building had entrances east and west consisting of broad white marble steps and massive dual wood doors. Motifs of arcane and obscure symbols and designs covered both. They had little graffiti but several dents from stones thrown at them. Orestes had spoken to Cyril about the incidences, but, lacking knowledge or parties deemed guilty of the crime, he got nowhere with the Patriarch.

Steps led down from the corner of the building and right turned into a maze of subterranean passageways. They made a series of quick turns until they reached Hypatia's study room. It was spacious, almost half the size of her lecture hall in the floor above. Everywhere books filled the shelves and papyrus rolls lay in pigeon holes and in stacks and piles. At first glance the room appeared disorganized, but closer examination showed that the books were very carefully ordered.

"Were all these rescued from the Serapeum, Hypatia?"

"Yes, father, but most ancient writings were hidden, as I said before. Many of the Gospels and writings of Jesus' disciples have also been hidden in and around Alexandria. With the help of Synesius, I have read several. Look at this scroll."

Theon moved closer to the ancient papyrus, cleaning his magnifying crystal absentmindedly with right thumb and forefinger and a fold of his white robe. He examined the edges of the scroll first.

"This is excellent material. I don't believe I've ever seen such quality!"

"It's over three thousand years old, father."

Theon's mouth dropped open as he turned to look at Hypatia. She could not suppress a laugh at his astonishment.

"Three thousand years?"

"At least. I haven't discovered a cript-code for any numerical expressions yet. I just found this yesterday. But, I do know the author."

"Who?"

"He whom the ancient priests worshipped as 'Thoth' or 'Tuti.' Consider the symbols inside this oval. The Ibis-headed man, the crescent moon, what appears to be a dog, and his tablet with lines and a dot. This is the signature of Thoth Hermes whom the ancients declared the Bringer of Writing and Letters to man. I've not deciphered much of it yet..."

Theon was now sitting in front of the scroll spread out on a low podium. He examined the hieroglyphs with excited intensity.

Shortly he exclaimed, "I've found the key!"

Hypatia leaned closer, placing her hands on Theon's shoulders.

He spoke again slowly, "The key is in the symbols of Thoth's name. The three dots in a triangle indicate that Thoth was not the original author. They point to the poem that precedes a story of another...see how they seem to point to these title glyphs at the top of this column. The opening poem then begins...it's about the end of Atlantis."

Theon solemnly read on,

"One Divine Flame

One Divine Flame, his robe sky blue and sun gold,
Master of tetractys wisdom,
walking the darkened labyrinth with initiate,
to him this story told...

Rich green emerald lands were once
where Seribis goes to dream,
in his heart lived the golden virtued.

Ages passed before Good gave birth to wrong,
Good saw good and longed for praise-
instead of pride conceited arrogance was born.

Soon the powerful few turned to war,
to conquer all, including what were once true
brothers,
only One there was who stood above them all,
on him the tides of war depend.

A son and lord named Azeus,
by peace and craft subdued,
the wicked half *and* passive,
great cheer before the loss of all.

The final end was known by some,
High Priests escaped to many lands,
the many from a source have come,
there being One Divine Flame."

There, Theon stopped. He looked up into
his daughter's gentle face. "This is an incredible

document, Hypatia. I knew the Gypsies had worshipped Serapis, whom Thoth calls Seribis, in the Serapeum. No doubt their Tarot hides the secrets of Thoth Hermes, the Thrice Blessed."

"Yes, father. They would have everyone think their cards are for games and fortune-telling, but it may save their sacred knowledge from Cyril's zealous Christians who would see all ancient wisdom destroyed."

Theon was again worried for his daughter. Any ancient, esoteric, or pagan knowledge was subject to Cyril's interpretation. Even different sects of Christians were open to attack. They almost always became labeled 'blasphemous' or 'heretic,' and therefore due whatever destruction the Patriarch deemed appropriate. The Nitrian monks were nothing more than an organized mob that carried out Cyril's orders. They were feared by all. Hypatia's voice brought Theon back from his thoughts.

"I think there is a common thread of facts and beliefs that has survived the ages. I see it run through the works of Plato, in ancient myths and stories, and I see and *feel* it anew in the true Christian way."

"What?"

"Plato in his Theaetetus said, 'The beginning thereof of the knowledge of the truth is to wonder at things.' Matthias has written in his 'Traditions' a warning to 'Wonder at what is present,' establishing this as the first step to the knowledge of those things beyond. Clement wrote of the saying in both their works over two hundred years ago. There were, and still are, Gnostic monks who claimed to have the Gospel, but I doubt very much it is the original. I know where the Gospel of Thomas is hidden. In it are many words of the Son of Man, Jesus, that are inherently pure and noble, so like the beliefs of great philosophers.

"I know this is dangerous to say, but Cyril and his monks are the furthest from what true Christians should be. Think to separate the words of Jesus from the pitiful dogma of Cyril's church, and you begin to see what He really taught and stood for. His act of selfless sacrifice contains within that great deed the noblest lesson of all. He has..."

"I've read parts of Thomas too, and the letters Synesius sent you about Phillip and others, remember? I think that we must study further these ancient scrolls, but be very secretive learning more about the teachings of Jesus through documents that are hunted and destroyed by jealous sects of 'Christians.' Perhaps Plutarch would be a wise source from which to draw knowledge of original writings of Jesus in Aramaic."

As they took in the aura of Hypatia's study with its hundreds of ancient scrolls illuminated by several large beeswax candles, a warmth engulfed them. It was a special, spiritual moment. But, while the feeling was energetic and good, somewhere in Theon's soul also burned a deeper feeling of empty loneliness.

Asclepe and Hypatia in Athens

Eventually, Theon and Asclepe convinced Hypatia of, at least, a longer vacation than she wanted. Preparations were made for their passage and soon the day came to leave. Many people saw them off or watched them from the busy docks. Merchants loaded and unloaded their wares, travelers from near and far, and soldiers both Roman and Goth went about their business after stealing a glance at Hypatia. Her fame and presence drew much attention. Theon smiled and waved as the sleek craft was pushed from its berth. He sighed a breath of relief. 'They would be safe in Athens,' thought Theon, 'May God be with her,' he said to himself as he turned and walked away. And so, there was a journey and a time in the ageless city of Athens.

·······

The setting sun glowed a golden hue on the port side of the craft. Her masters called her Phoceni, and thought of it as alive, having a spirit of her own. They worshipped the trim three sail vessel not as an idol, but a representation of the Creator's success in instilling perfection in a physical thing. The 'pagans' were peaceful and mild in their way of life, and wished no harm to Nature and humanity. But, many of the Roman Christians still had the inherent desire for war, and some waged it viciously against creeds of different interpretations. So, the ship's owner and captain kept their devotions to her operation and safe travel private.

The half-sun on their left painted the skies and sails orange, and at its setting drew a dark red line along the horizon. Stars began to twinkle as they came to life in the ever darkening skies. A few shone fuzzy behind two or three faint wisps of high feathery clouds as sails whistled their songs in the chill wind. Evening brought a cooling over the deep waters of the Mediterranean Sea.

·······

"More cheese or bread, Hypatia?"

"No, dear, I will finish this last fig and sip my wine, I'm full."

"Isn't it wonderful to glide across the waters, and to travel to far lands? I wish I could go to India or to England. Why don't we spend the rest of our years traveling?"

"I would like that, Asclepe, but my home will always be in Alexandria. Do you know what I secretly dream?"

"No."

"That I could meet one of the Christian Apostles, Paul, or most of all, Jesus. But, they were of yesterday, and gone is their bright glory, ever fading in the destruction and altering of the Christian religion. I find only partial satisfaction in learning of them, much like the fragments of their writings, sometimes they merely give clues to their former selves. I find knowledge in the sayings of Thomas, but they lack the passion of the other Gospels of Matthew, Mark, or John. Paul describes the mechanics of Christianity in his letters to different churches he founded, and the rules for a holy and worthy life."

Over the last few months, Asclepe became more and more interested in learning of the Christian religion, not from Cyril, but from Hypatia, and from what little some Gnostic friends told her. As with everyone, she loved to talk with Hypatia. It was more than becoming mesmerized at her lectures, their lifelong friendship meant that they shared a private wealth of knowledge and learning. They could talk about anything in a family bond as close as sisters. Although she lived with her father in Athens more than Hypatia, they basically grew up together and were never apart for more than a few years.

Asclepe had silver wisps at each temple to accent short dark brown hair. Auburn highlights could be seen when she walked in bright sunlight. Her light-olive shade skin gave away an Athenian birthplace, and a classic Grecian form confirmed it, though she was not considered tall at only five foot four, but petite. She loved to do domestic things for Hypatia, and often cooked or mended clothes, or ran other errands for her and Theon.

Her curiosity soon took hold, and she looked up at her traveling companion. "Before we left Alexandria I was speaking with a friend of mine, I don't think you know him, about the epistles of Paul. Don't you find it strange that as Saul, he persecuted so many of the new Christian Cult? And yet, he became their leading spokesman."

"There are many things about Christianity that puzzle me, and yet, if we separate Truth from the creative writing of the Gospel narratives, an amazing thing happens. Let me explain.

"The author of the Christian Gospel of Luke and the writer of the Acts of the Apostles are one, of course, and it seems he accompanied Paul on most of his journeys. He sought to portray the beginnings of Christianity in a historical framework, despite, or perhaps because of, the obvious hindrance of secondhand information regarding the life of Jesus. His works are the most erudite of all the Gospels, and this is fitting, for an attempt to capture history accurately is the most difficult of literary disciplines. Although his Gospel was derived from recycled oral experience and tradition, one can say that it is supported, at least in part, from his firsthand experiences with Paul. Remember, Hebrew tradition and lore is handed down with legendary accuracy, though its stories are written with allegory, parable, and metaphor to emphasize their point.   Hence numbers, for example, can play a role in representing ideas or familiarity with other traditions, even though their historical accuracy may be lacking foundation in fact. One can argue whether this makes any difference in the overall picture. Did it really rain for forty days and nights in the Flood Myths, did the Jews wander for exactly forty years in the desert, did Jesus fast for forty days after His baptism by John? Although legend may prophesy history, or vice versa, none-the-less, the significance of the number forty holds deeper, sometimes mysterious meaning. Luke seems to take pride in exacting the truest history in his narratives, and he is reluctant in using hyperbole or symbols for effect. I think he *must* have had access to the earliest of written sources, possibly Aramaic in language, though nothing survives to this day. Perhaps all the original writings of the times were destroyed in the Roman sack and destruction of Jerusalem shortly before Luke's written gospels. The dates seem right."

"I find his experience with Paul in Athens fascinating. Do you remember the story of the unknown God? "

"Yes, it took place at the Aeropagus, where the supreme Court of Athens meets. The Romans call it Mars Hill. Didn't your father tell us this story when we were children? Even before we knew of the Christian authors?"

"Yes. It was my first interest in learning of them."

"Mine too," Hypatia agreed, "Plutarch no doubt started me on my road to learning of Christianity through that story. It is one of Paul's most famous sermons, you know. Theon loved it too. He read it recently and called Paul the first Christian philosopher because of the style and manner in which he spoke to the Athenians."

"Paul was very clever. No doubt he saw the many statues and temples devoted to the pantheon of pagan gods. He must have been overwhelmed at the idolatry. Especially having a Hebrew upbringing and then eventually being born again as a Christian. Monotheism was central to his beliefs for his entire life, and then presented before him is the picture that more gods live in Athens than men!

"How clever to begin his presentation at the marketplace to Epicurean and Stoic philosophers eager to learn of and worship all gods." Asclepe paused a second and then added, "At least to show no deity disrespect."

"The unknown God," Hypatia mused. " The Athenian philosophers honored Paul by allowing him an opening, and he used their curiosity wisely in his sermon to them. "

"Yes, and then he introduced the power of God by stating that by Him all things were created. All things could be seen as proof of His invisible existence. All things were made through Him and for Him. God's omnipresence was stressed in Paul's second point."

"Paul finished his sermon," Hypatia concluded, "with the proof of man's salvation through the resurrection of Jesus. The Lord's suffering and crucifixion were for the sins of mankind, and all who realize this would be saved at the final judgment. All who acknowledge Him and work righteousness are accepted by Him."

"Some sneered at the talk of resurrection, saying they had heard of it before, but others would ask for more information and eventually become followers," Asclepe finished.

Constellations were now glittering against dark skies as small waves lapped alongside the gliding sailing ship. A cool, soft wind filled the sails silently, letting the slapping waves beat a steady tattoo in its turn. Starlight gleamed with its soft hues on billowed canvas as the captain of the Phoceni checked her stays and ties along the mast poles and jib poles. Everything was working smoothly on the craft as her captain took a break to check on its special passengers.

"Good evening ladies. Can I get you anything?"

"The food and drink were wonderful, thank you captain."

"Asclepe...," he bowed, "And you, daughter of Theon, anything you wish? I am at your service."

"No thank you, captain. Will you join us? "

"My conversation might be boring to you both, Phoceni's owner says I speak too much of politics, and not enough philosophy."

"Politics is a Philosophy of its own and no less interesting sir," Asclepe replied, then added, "Our discussions of religious beliefs may be boring to you."

"Some would see the two married again, only for power, and not as the golden age of times long gone," Hypatia frowned.

"Well, take Orestes for example." He looked at his audience side-long, as if to await an answer that this was a proper topic. The last thing he wanted to do was insult the daughter of Theon!

"The man is an enigma," Hypatia responded, "yet his complexity may be due in part to the several roles he plays. He is 'Roman Prefect,' and tries to balance forces against each other in hopes of civil peace. He tolerates the Jews, though a self-proclaimed Christian, yet he and Cyril are enemies within their faith. The Gnostics are all but at war with Cyril. In the center of all this, the Visigoths wander about while at treaty with Rome looking for territory to settle in.

"Rational minds are merely witnesses to this grand play, we as philosophers stand almost alone in our quest for peace. Ironically, our best allies might often be found with the Roman foot soldier turned true Christian. Some soldiers have been very Heroic in their attempts to follow their Lord's way rather than their captains'."

"I know of many stories of the catacombs of Rome," the captain added. "The escape from persecutions, tortures. It is said that Nero had Christians tied to stakes, doused with oil, and set ablaze as human torches to light the nights." He hung his head in shame that a human would do that to a fellow man.

He was known as 'the Captain' and not by any other name, but he was well-liked, and respected for both knowledge and opinion. His grey beard was full but trimmed. Eyes, saddened from his thoughts, carried a shine when his head turned up to the skies. The captain wiped his eyes with the back of his hand and checked on star positions as part of his navigational duties. They were on course.

"I wish that all men had your compassion, Captain." Asclepe gently massaged his shoulder attempting to comfort him.

"Please be careful when we reach Athens, ladies. Former pagan shrines are being converted to Christian churches, and should be avoided. Many have been abandoned or gone underground."

"What of Delphi?"

He turned to Hypatia, "The Delphic oracle is closed and abandoned, but safe from monks for now because of the difficulty getting to it. The climb up Mount Parnassus preserves its isolation. The monks think it is totally abandoned, and certain Roman authorities assure them of it. Guests of Plutarch are safe, he has many contacts, and all treat him with respect. You will be safe in your journey, but be careful."

The night was filled with the sounds of constant waves and winds. Stars and moonlight glistened and danced off the sparkling sea.

It was a while before anyone spoke again. The captain had excused himself when relieved by a crewman. He retired to his cabin below deck.

Asclepe and Hypatia both said goodnight about a half-hour later, and also went below to their respective cabins to a sound and peaceful rocking sleep.

The days passed in sun and smooth sailing for the Phoceni and her passengers. She carried a cargo of fine figs and other products of Alexandria all stored in fired clay pots, even the bolts of cloth rolled and standing upright over the tops of four large pots. The hold was full, and when they finally landed at the docks there was little time for lengthy goodbyes. The crew and captain began unloading her cargo even as dock workers tied lines from bow and stern to dock-posts. There were many perishables that needed attention. Even still, they watched them disembark and leave, fully aware that their most precious cargo had just left the ship.

· · · · · · ·

"Hypatia! Now don't you agree our souls are being born again even as we retrace this road from quay to town. Beloved Athens, how we've missed you so!"

Hypatia didn't answer Asclepe, but looked from side to side. She was looking for something missing, and wondered what it was as she hurried to catch the exuberant Asclepe. As they walked north towards the 'Double Gate' of Athens, where four highways converged, they passed through an extensive cemetery where many distinguished citizens where buried. Asclepe was running, almost flying, as if death were releasing her bonds to earth and all its material concerns, and in youthful glee, her spirit was experiencing rebirth in a new, glorious world.

"Asclepegenia, sister of rationality, you are like a child chasing a butterfly. Slow down and let me catch up to you."

"I'm sorry...but I must warn you, by the time I reach the Acropolis I will be impossible with excitement!"

"Dear Asclepe, you would never be intolerable. Your innocence and life bring happiness to my soul. Atop the Athenian plain, when morning sings its songs tomorrow, you must do your gazing into Heaven's blue skies."

"I will. I wish you could come with me, we could play on flute and lyre in celebration and praise of this, the city of my soul and youth. But, you must go to my father, I know...and what a noble man he is, and a great philosopher...and handsome."

Hypatia was surprised at the pixie grin on her friend's face accompanying her last words. She laughed easily and gently pushed her.

They walked for awhile beside the long low rock walls that led to Athens, enjoying the pastoral countryside. On a slope to the left a flock of sheep grazed on the rich green hillsides. The slope twisted and climbed ever upwards from the Bay of Phaleron behind them. The deep blue Gulf of Aegina now lay farther below, but still contained a powerful peace in its size. They stopped to rest and take in its beauty.

"Too soon we will be at the Cephesus River. I'm glad we stopped here. We can rest for awhile and talk before we part. What's wrong Hypatia? Is it just that I'm overexcited, or do I detect some somber mood?"

"I'm sorry, Asclepe, I don't want to dampen your jubilance, but a foreboding feeling grips my soul."

"Perhaps it's just all the tension and strain of living in Alexandria that has been *released* from your soul." Hypatia knew better, but said nothing. "When you see my father he will also tell you so, I'm sure. I will join you at his school in a few days."

They spent an hour trading small talk and gazing into the sea and sky. Then they parted, Asclepe walking along the wall to Athens, Hypatia going east along the Cephesus River. While she walked, Asclepe reveled in the scenery, but Hypatia pondered deeply. She thought to herself, "I must seek the oracle before I visit Plutarch."

Suddenly Hypatia realized what was missing, what worried her. There were no philosophers at the quays or on the roads! She recalled the many wandering philosophers speaking their sometimes eloquent beliefs wherever one would listen. They were missing! Even in times of war they were ever present, but now they were gone. Had the Christians finally chased away every living pagan philosopher? Hypatia carried mixed emotions of worry and anger in her thoughts. Her pace quickened for the oracle. It would be almost a day's ride by chariot and then a half-day climb up Mount Parnassus.

Hypatia finally stepped down from the rented chariot, her mention of Plutarch enough to secure its lease from a stable near the Cephesus. She walked around to the chestnut colored horse and pet his nose.

"You are a fine horse, Equetes, thank you."

She handed the reins to a waiting boy who would groom and feed his master's horse before returning it to him.

He spoke timidly, "Excuse me for intruding upon your thoughts..." He waited for a reply to continue his conversation.

She looked at the young man, an adolescent, fourteen or fifteen, but mature looking for his age. Short black curly hair topped his five foot frame. Hypatia looked down into an olive skinned face. His eyes were large, brown, and hid what the serious look on his face could not. Lines of concern wrinkled his forehead and caused a tightness in his cheeks and jaw line. Despite feelings of trust for the young man, she wished to remain anonymous. After some thought she spoke.

"Who am I to speak to the keeper of such a fine horse? I am a hand maiden about my father's business."

She motioned shyly with the toe of her right foot on the ground, tracing the symbol of a fish with two curved lines intersecting to form a tail. This was the ancient secret symbol of the true Christians, traced in places where open admission to the sect could quickly cause persecution, accusations of heresy, and often death.

"Thank you for a sign, you choose your words well in these times. Plutarch has many friends in this area, yet, even so, it is wise to remain inconspicuous. The two day climb from here keeps many away, though, in the cities many of our brothers and sisters are killed for their beliefs. It is hard for me to understand why certain Christians wage war on people who where born with different ideas of God. Followers of the Nicaean edict would even brand their own countrymen as heretics if they do not conform. The Gnostics are persecuted in Alexandria, are they not?"

"Yes, but our Prefect uses no force against them. It is all the work of Cyril's monks that cause strife. Yet, they are cautious in their opinions of Roman power. What they don't know is that many Roman soldiers are secretly devout Christians, and are tolerant concerning religion. They are peaceful, though they put on a strong face of authority. Alexandria is a storm of politics between civil and 'church,' each vying for absolute top position in the eyes of man and God. We are but philosophers and teachers, not much more than observers, with little say in events unfolding."

The young man was hypnotized by her beauty and poise. Women in Athens were made 'second' in the scheme of things, by rules of church and state, and were forced to act that way. To the ward of Plutarch, Hypatia was no less than a mother goddess, coming home to claim back her philosophers and followers.

"Plutarch himself asked me to be here when you return. I am at your service."

"Then, you know who I am?"

"Yes. I will await your return."

"Thank you, what is your name?"

"I am Sophacles."

Hypatia began the long climb, following a well worn path up a gentle slope. As she turned to the right past a hill, the youth's gaze switched to the road below. No one followed. If necessary, he was prepared to die to protect Plutarch's guest.

As he began to unfasten chariot from horse, he muttered profanities directed at the powerful leaders of Roman Christianity. No one but Constantine's dead soul and the horse heard him.

She continued up the side of Mount Parnassus as the incline gradually became steeper then leveled again before rising up another southwestern slope. The plain was about a thousand feet wide with only one well worn trail across the sometimes patchy green lawn. A flock of sheep grazed on tufts of dark green grass as one scratched itself against a lone olive tree. A shepherd humbly watched a single figure walk up the path to the oracle, still another half-day away.

By the end of the day Hypatia had reached her goal. A large stone building with many small rooms sat just off the path. Tired from the climb, she went inside, selected a room, made absolutions, and quickly fell asleep.

The sun had not yet fully emerged in clear blue skies the next morning, but wanting to get an early start, Hypatia arose, stretched, and left the stone lodge. She drew deep breathes of fresh mountain air, then remembered the sweet, perfumed air of the oracle. It lay less than a half-day's walk ahead. Then she would wait for her turn to enter.

She began the last ascent to Pytho, now named the Oracle of Delphos, the womb. At mid-day she reached the cave's entrance, a narrow crack in the side of Parnassus mountain. Thick brush all but hid its portal. An old man sat on a large stone before the cave. He had a white cloth tied at the back of his head and pulled down over his eyes. He leaned on a cane with two wrinkled and long fingered hands. Hypatia heard the sulfur gases escaping in long exaggerated hisses and instantly smelled the pleasant vapors.

The old man spoke loudly, "The great serpent tells you to go, leave here or he will swallow you up."

Hypatia was unmoved. "I have been here before, old man, though I don't remember you."

"I have been here for many years and have never seen you either."

"Is time then merely a recollection of what one experiences?"

"There is no time here. If you seek time, go to Athens, forget this place."

"I will wait, seeking neither time nor timelessness. I have been here before, as you know."

"I'm warning you, if by old age I die, my ghost will not let you pass. You may as well leave now and spend your youth in other more productive pursuits."

Hypatia had played a question and answer game the last time she visited the oracle over twenty-five years ago. Only then, it was more riddles and philosophical preponderances for the visitor. Now, it was warnings, plain and simple. Hypatia was saddened by the change, and it provoked a determination in her to see the oracle. She would not come this far only to turn away in fear. The gatekeeper's admonitions became a test of patience. She would wait and clear her mind.

Theodisus had closed the Delphic oracle, in fact all oracles were subject to confiscation and destruction or conversion into churches in the typical brutal fashion of Rome. The oracle at Delphi was remote, and so divinations continued in secret, and much less frequently. Christianity had been the official religion of Rome since the time of Constantine, but the philosophers and scholars of Pagan religions coexisted with Rome in those times. Theodisus had gone to war against and defeated the last remnant of pagan Roman soldiers in the Battle of the Frigidus, two years after the Serapeum was ordered destroyed in Alexandria. He was a strong believer in the Nicene Christians, and had even given non-Nicene churches away to followers of his creed. He died almost two decades ago, thought Hypatia, yet the impetus of struggle for power remains. For many years it had been bubbling like soup in a cauldron in Alexandria. But, the Nicene Christians were going to win, even if it meant taking their share then spilling the rest.

A four foot round, flat-topped boulder made a convenient place to rest from the late afternoon sun. The shade was rare at that time of the day, and Hypatia welcomed it. The old man continued to sit in the sun.

The afternoon passed quickly and evening's dusk began.

A crescent moon glowed an ivory yellow in the still hazy dark blue skies. As the twilight appeared below the glowing moon, Hypatia looked towards the gatekeeper. He was gone.

The Delphic Oracle

Wandering to the narrow entrance, Hypatia peaked inside the dark, ancient cavern. From the opening, ever broader steps led down and around a turn to the left. Part of a landing could be seen. A tripod with a bowl of burning oil atop its frame illuminated the landing and its surrounding walls. The flame danced easily in the nearly breezeless passageway. Hypatia stepped inside and at once became aware of a strong fume. She swooned in the intoxicating gasses and became numb in her extremities. Carefully descending the stone staircase hewn out of solid rock ages ago, she struggled to maintain a clear mind and balance.

Secrets and mysteries, edges of reality and fantasy- Hypatia found that she saw things as long ago when younger. A child's panorama opened before her eyes. Subtle lights burst into displays of sounds and sights, in meanings that were real. Crevices too small to crawl into became huge halls of homes to myriad creatures, some tiny and terrible. She smiled with youthful happiness as numerous myths and monsters came to life in a kaleidoscope of memories. Previous fears disappeared.   Moments of patient waiting and watching lingered and blended with a child's reality.   Eventually she began to wonder if there was anyone else in the room.   She looked about, but wasn't sure.   The doubt raised hairs of fear on the back of her neck and forearms.

Seeing the entire cavern in slow motion made her realize everything in past, present, and future all at once.   She remembered her previous trip to the Oracle as the perfumed fumes escaped from narrow fissures leading to the main chamber in groans and hisses.   Soon the child's view was gone and Hypatia stood in the adyton before the oracle. Its holy man was standing opposite, about fifteen feet away, recording everything the entranced priestess said or did.

Garbed in simple white flowing robe, a garnet of white and lavender wild flowers adorned her head.   Long black hair hung in loosely braided ropes to her hips.   She was sitting in the center of her audience suspended in the air above the wide fissure holding a sprig of laurel in her right hand and a cup in the other.   From the base of her tripod, three long legs ending in claws gripped the rim around the fathomless pit.

While standing before the oracle, the holy man standing opposite recorded. There was a calm awe surrounding the priestess. Try as she might, Hypatia could not speak to ask of her any question. She concentrated again and again until rivulets of sweat ran down her forehead and temples, but speech would not come. The sybil rambled in an unknown tongue as the holy man struggled to interpret the meaning of her words. The priest-scribe helped Hypatia outside, and, after sitting her down, fumbled to straighten the notes he had taken during the divination.

She whispered to the priest,
"From times of old when deeds were gold,
The Serpent swayed and souls delayed
their ways across the Pythian Plain.
Then one was born with royal horn,
Man at birth, sun child of Earth,
subdued and willed Pytho to tell.
Apollo of Jupiter, Mother Latona and muse,
Manchild of Moon, Ea's healing boon
named mighty Pytho to proclaim.
In vengeance and greed of His honorable deed,
Pytho in chaos proclaimed and exclaimed,
that only ordained may declare or decree."

Hypatia was sitting on the same rock as before. The priest-scribe had been held by her voice, and now the two looked at each other. Green eyes sparkling with energy and purity, nowhere in the clear night sky did there gleam more precious diamonds. The white-robed priest-scribe was quite awestruck by her. He stood motionless, his folded hands at his chest. It seemed that he did not move them, but rather, an unseen force released the gravity in his arms so that they were lifted upwards to a pinnacle above his head. His hands and arms then unfolded in a fan to his sides. Eventually, they returned to form a cross at his chest.

An aura surrounded them both, its moonlight glow laced like a fine ivory veil when the Priest spoke in a mesmerizing voice,

"I am the Alpha and Omega, bring this word back to you:
Virgo, your curiosity brings you to ask,
that you complete your enlightened task,
and Ea surely cries from sorrow and joyed.
That everywhere your courage be employed,
Pure Truth never wearing shame for a mask,
Light and Life in brilliant Love We will bask."

A vigorous breath of wonderful peace filled them both, making them feel light-headed, happy. The silver- haired priest smiled and bowed slightly to Hypatia. Tears quickly welled in his eyes.

"Thank you. Your grace has been with us twice in thrice-filled bliss. I will mourn the loss of your presence much, and for long times, and will survive only by the memory of this experience that now embraces us."

Her eyes moistened, but to her delicate ears the priest's gaze was drawn. It was to the holy man her subtle way of saying, "I hear."

Many hours of joy and refreshing peace filled them. They sat in the temple built for Initiates to meditate and learn in. Much was given at the divinations in the form of hidden knowledge, too esoteric to learn but by direct experience, and only later through reflection. Five in all filled the room at first, then later many others joined them. They talked through the night of wondrous things, but there was no mention of Hypatia's divinations.

Dawn greeted the sylvan hills and rocky ridges of Mount Parnassus. The first light was a rich dark red that lasted only brief minutes before bursting into pinks and golds. It was a spectacular, colorful sunrise.

At mid-afternoon, Hypatia left. She walked the same path taken by many others who had come to the oracle at Delphi. And, as had the many others, she too returned to her destiny enlightened by the voice of ages.

Plutarch, Asclepe and Hypatia

It was early evening and warm breezes were rising from the Mediterranean. The air was filled with myriad scents of different types of blossoms and buds. Below the plateau on which Plutarch's home was built were groves of olive trees. Dragon flies were chasing mosquitoes, bees were hurrying to their hives loaded with precious nectar, and far-away clouds were drawing an orange and russet curtain on the western skies. Evening oil lamps were lit by young students around a patio at the back of the large stone home that also served as Plutarch's school. Drinks of mineral water, almond syrup, and lemon were being served as they sat at massive round marble tables.

"The skies are magnificent, Hypatia, your stay has surely influenced the beauty of the natural wonders around us."

"I appreciate your kindness and hospitality, as well as this refreshing drink, Plutarch. Thank you."

Plutarch was a model Athenian. He was in his late sixties, but an austere diet and vigorous mental and physical exercise had preserved his health well. He walked extensively throughout the countryside and had many friends far and wide. Soothsayers and beggars, tutor to Kings, physician to farmer; Plutarch the Younger was respected and admired by all.

"Your presence honors me Hypatia, but I will agree, this is a fine school with many adept young philosophers. But, I would like to change the subject and ask you what you thought of your visit to the oracle?"

Hypatia's mood abruptly changed to one of chagrin. She turned back to the west as the last orange-gold drop of sun slipped quietly from view. On cue, evening insects began their chirps and whirrs, a cacophony of sounds against the approaching dark silence of night.

Still facing west she spoke, "...the stars begin to shine, just as the teachings of the Master begin to appear to my understanding. This new religion of Christianity will spread throughout the world, I only pray that the Truths in its fundamental teachings will not be lost."

"It is ironic that rather than love one another in fellowship, they squabble over doctrines, even to *killing* one another!" Plutarch showed his disgust, then in a caring tone added, "Why don't you stay with us? You can continue your work here, safe in my school. I worry for you. Alexandria is a bubbling caldron."

"Fear not, I am safe for now, yet, death will never kill the soul nor spirit. We have pledged ourselves to Truth, and by truth we shall live. The resurrection of Jesus is proof, I am convinced, of our roles in the Heavens' after life, after all we do on earth in His name. His teachings have been so corrupted by Cyril and others like him...it amazes me. Compassion, Love, and Goodness fill His teachings. In like manner He is filled with wisdom, knowledge, and philosophy. How can Cyril and others so debase His ideals with their actions?"

"I am not unfamiliar with the pure Christian ways. We have many friends who follow Him in heart and spirit, not in unconscious greed and lust for power and prominence. These traveling Christians speak with us and we listen very closely. We can hear and understand their words, often communicating with them in our own language though they speak in foreign tongues. They tell us of the Christos, spirit of the Son, descending from the Heavens upon Jesus of Nazareth. And that since His death, He lives with us on earth. We often experience His life and energy."

"Are they nearby? Can I meet them?"

Hypatia spoke with the enthusiasm of adolescence, sending Plutarch back in time. She spent many years in Athens in his home, and though not his child, she was like a daughter to him. Hypatia's father, Theon, was not related to him, but they were strongly associated in mutual studies and philosophies, and life-time friends.

"Yes, perhaps I can arrange a meeting. Give me a couple of days."

There was a long pause.

"The oracle said that I can neither escape nor alter my destiny. And yet, I feel that I must. There is something that I have to do before my time comes. His teachings are ancient seeds blooming from the life in His love for all. I *must* have more time!"

Plutarch was no longer totally visible. His robe remained white, simple, tied with a thin purple sash at his waist. His head, his folded arms, and his sandaled feet were sometimes flesh-toned, sometimes reflections of starlight, and sometimes Plutarch the Younger was invisible.

"You don't need to go back," Plutarch said softly.

"I cannot stay my good friend. Before I left Alexandria I learned a certain news. A library council has given me Theon's chair in philosophy. Father first thought it a good idea, then feared the jealousies and ignorance of the monks of Cyril."

"I would wish you here, teacher and more in this school."

"I don't wish to turn from that honor, but I must. There are things to record for posterity, and I do wish to return to Alexandria. I will be safe so long as Orestes is Prefect."

They both enjoyed the evening's starry splendor, and said little more.

....

Sunrise took the last chill of night from the air as Hypatia awoke. The guest room was in the eastern corner of Plutarch's home, and had a spectacular view of the eastern skies. Goats had already been milked and were out grazing underneath the olive trees and pastures further from the house. The dewy lawns glistened in morning sun that was blooming in pinks and creamy tangerines. A pitcher of cool water and a large clay bowl sat on a table by Hypatia's bed. She arose and poured water in the bowl, then splashed some on her face with cupped hands. The water was invigorating and took the last trace of sleep from her eyes. Today Asclepe was to meet with Hypatia and Plutarch, her father. Thought of their reunion pleased Hypatia, she knew her father was excited to see her again as well, though he made sure to treat all his guests equally. He was a superb host, and even now breakfast was almost ready, its fragrant cooking odors wafting through his home.

Dining was done outside on the patio when weather allowed, and the eastern skies were filled with the sun's fully risen energy. Hypatia walked out to the warm courtyard and took a seat at one of its stone tables. Plutarch and a young student soon appeared carrying trays with assorted fruits and cheeses, a basket with warm loaves and cups, and a fine porcelain pitcher of fresh goat's milk. Plutarch gave each a cup and placed the loaves on the table. The student put the pitcher of milk and fruit and cheese trays in the center next to the bread.

"Jason, will you say our prayer for Hypatia?"

"Yes, sir. This is a prayer of the Christians I have learned from the followers of Mary Magdalene, the disciple whom Jesus loved. It was she who is author of the original Aramaic Gospel of John."

Plutarch reached out and took hold of Hypatia's and Jason's hand, and after a moment of silence, Jason spoke.

"Our Heavenly Father, Hallowed is Your name.

Your Kingdom is come.

Your will is done, as in heaven so also on earth.

Give us the bread for our daily need.

And leave us serene, just as we also allowed others serenity. And do not pass us through trial, except separate us from the evil one.

For Yours is the Kingdom, the Power and the Glory to the end of the universe, of all the universes. Amen!"

"Amen!" Plutarch and Hypatia said together.

"What a wonderful morning, Plutarch. That was a beautiful prayer, Jason. Thank you- well spoken."

"The Lord's Prayer," Jason said serenely.

"The dear Apostle Mary's words are so hidden and belittled, I thought you would enjoy some knowledge of her if you were so inclined." He blurted his words out, but then spoke looking down, "Pardon my bad manners, I meant no insult, your wisdom and knowledge is legendary in Athens, as is your noble father's."

"No insult taken. I am fascinated by the religion and wish to gather all I can to take back with me to Alexandria. Many of the original manuscripts have either been hidden or destroyed. As the solidification of the Christian church takes place, it would please its founder if it were based on His teachings to the original Disciples. Among these I knew Mary had played a major, perhaps original role, but I did not now that she wrote the Gospel of John. You have evidence of this?"

Hypatia took a piece of flat pita bread as Plutarch broke off a piece of a small loaf and handed Jason the rest. All took pieces of fruit and cheese.

"Logic more than evidence, so that the early years remain mysterious and secretive. Perhaps that is why there is so much argument and battle over dogma, though those that fight are those that would alter the truth and spread dissent for their own ends. The Truth is in the Lord's words, not church creed."

"I agree. His words are so logical and righteous. My students all believe in the Master Jesus, as do I," Plutarch emphasized with a nod. "We cherish the equality of women here, though almost everywhere else they are second rated and not treated with the same respect."

"The Gnostics in Alexandria treat us with dignity."

"There are many who know the teachings of Mary, Thomas, and Matthias among the Gnostics. But, be careful what you seek, many male leaders in the growing Christian church would subjugate or punish women for what they might deem heresy."

"I know, I deal with it all the time back home." Hypatia took another small bite of bread. "Fortunately, father and I have many friends, both in the Library and in the city. I will be discreet. I would hear more of your theory, Jason."

"Do you know of Oxyrhynchus, Jason?" Plutarch interrupted.

"No."

Hypatia added, "I only know of the Library there, we don't travel much outside of Alexandria, except now." She smiled at Plutarch, "You are a wonderful host to enlighten our souls. Please tell us."

"The Gospel of Mary Magdalene was written in Aramaic, originally, as was the Gospel of Thomas, and was secreted in the Library at Alexandria for a time, translated to Greek, and then the copies sent to Oxyrhynchus. They were then hidden in a dump after the Library there was ordered to destroy all 'non-Nicean' approved papyri, and resides there safely for now, papyri in clay pots."

"Tragic that knowledge is so debased that extraordinary attempts must be made to save it. I think that this is my role in Alexandria, Plutarch. Knowledge must be saved."

"The Apostles tried," Jason added to the discussion. "There were papyri destroyed by the Romans in the early wars written by Mary in Aramaic. She was the 'beloved disciple,' whom many now think was John."

"There are many men who rank high in the church who fear even the *equality* of women," Plutarch said sadly. "In our midst is the torch of enlightenment. It seems to have been passed from Mary to you Hypatia- I pray for your safety."

"Thank you, Plutarch."

There was an awkward silence. Hypatia's thoughts were abstract, fearless, and indestructible. Knowledge, learning, and the confidence of Truth chased away her fears. Her world was grounded in the science of things and not raw human jealousies and ignorance. But, passion and compassion filled her lectures and drew her students to near worship her, and more important, to knowledge. Now there was a higher calling. She not only taught all those who would listen, but would preserve all she could for posterity.

·······

Later in the afternoon, the sun's lazy haze filled the olive groves with golden shafts of sunlight dazzling in the trees' leaves. The glittering bristled in the tree-tops with each easy zephyr arising from the slopes below Plutarch's home and school. Hypatia watched from her window. Plutarch and the house staff prepared to greet Asclepe. There was an air of excitement in the house in anticipation of her arrival, and a special dinner was being prepared to celebrate her return.

It was mid-afternoon when Asclepe finally arrived. Hypatia was back on the patio with Jason and Hermes sharing stuffed olives, cheeses and lemon flavored mineral water. They were discussing the writings of Mary Magdalene when Plutarch and Asclepe walked hand in hand from the house.

"She is here, safe and sound!"

"Hypatia! It is good to see you after these many days!"

"You as well. How was Athens?"

"Filled with beauty and majesty, but the monks are everywhere and often quarrel with those they have not yet converted to Christianity. Many mystery centers and pagan temples have been destroyed or taken over by the state run church. I'm glad Delphi was safe for you."

"Yes, I encountered no one and had no problems. Will you join us? We were just discussing the Gospel of Mary."

"I will bring you some lemonade, dear. Can I freshen yours, Hypatia? Jason? Hermes?"

"Yes, thank you," they all said at once.

As Plutarch left on his errand, Jason politely waited for a moment to make sure Hypatia and Asclepe had nothing else to say. He then continued.

"Mary Magdalene wrote in her Gospel of the Nature of things and life after death. She has told of the Lord's secret teachings and how He taught that all nature, all formations, and all creatures exist in and with one another, yet matter is resolved into the roots of its own nature.

"Mary also spoke of the Lord being in each and every one that believes, and that those who seek Him will find Him."

"This matches the Gnostic's belief," added Hypatia.

"The Gnostics realize that she was the great inspiration for the Lord's disciples. When they were desponded and afraid to teach the Gospel, she bolstered their spirits. Through her the Lord taught secrets of the mind, soul, and spirit. He explained that the mind is between the soul and the spirit, and that one who sees visions through the mind is at the door of truth and manifestation. Jesus also spoke through her to describe His ascension into the higher realms once His life on earth was ended. The final words in Mary's Gospel spoke of the admonition the Lord gave to not lay down any rule or law beyond what He had said. At this point the Disciples separated and began to preach the Gospel."

"That was wonderful, Jason. Tell us more."

"Excuse me, Jason, Hypatia, I must go help father with the dinner preparations. I understand that he is making quite a meal. Do not let me interrupt your teachings, Jason. Hypatia will fill me in later."

"Of course," the young man replied as he stood and lightly bowed."

•••••••

It was several days later when Plutarch said his farewells to Hypatia and his daughter Asclepe. Later, with passage booked and all aboard, the long, sleek boat, 'Evening Star' set sail for Alexandria.

Many times over the next days Hypatia and Asclepe took advantage of sunny skies and warm breezes, often lounging above-deck. Discussions filled the mornings and afternoons, and sometimes concluded below-deck into the night. Many of their conversations included religion as well as mathematics. Asclepe usually propounded the theory that all religion, by its very nature, was without rational origin. Only 'organizers' of its doctrines were followed, most often, and the Deity Himself, or Herself, became obscure, veiled in myth and traditions. Therefore, no one religion could serve man. Hypatia was more convinced that a science of religion was possible, since all creeds contain similar tenants. Yet, just as the Gnostics believed, she too felt the secret door to God opened from within. The way to its glory was being tested by the dictates of the Roman Church-state who would have all humanity find salvation through them only. Through the 'Church.' The words of Jesus rang true on so many counts, His gentle Spirit had brought not only peace and enlightenment, but, the sword of war to those who would use it. Many corrupt elect of the church-state of Rome wished to wield the scepter of religious authority over the masses. It was a dark and depressing time for those who had beliefs other than those of the official religion of Rome; a cloud was forming over the civilized world. Ironically, many were throwing down the sword and walking into the true light of a new emerging philosophy of Jesus, the founder of Christianity. Hypatia considered herself a recent convert, yet had lost nothing of her enlightenment and knowledge of 'pagan' philosophies.

They spent many hours in discussion during their voyage to Alexandria. One afternoon, as the sun climbed to its zenith against a cloudless blue sky, talk turned to the oracle's divinations.

"Father said the oracle praised your ambitions. This is a noble honor."

After a moments pause, Hypatia spoke, "Your father asked me to stay at his school, that was a noble honor, but, the chair of Philosophy that awaits me in Alexandria is a duty. It may be that I can remove my studies and documents to Athens, I must explore that possibility."

"Why wouldn't you wait in Athens and send for your studies and work?"

"Asclepegenia, what makes you speak of this subject again so quickly? Does our nearness to Alexandria worry you? We discussed this days before, remember?"

She did, but she said nothing.

"I must admit, a certain euphoria fills me when I think of the possibilities of uniting the ancient traditions with the teachings of Master Jesus. The old and the new must create a new age. We might not live long enough to see its full blossom, but just think, Asclepe, all the beauty of the ancients' sacred teachings glorified with the passionate wisdom of Jesus. Surely, in Him a Divine being has descended from the very Heavens. The Son of God."

So eloquent were Hypatia's words, so filled with joy was her spirit, Asclepe found nothing to say in return. She felt first and foremost that Hypatia was happy, but, underneath lay her deepest fear. She tried her hardest not to let it grow, though it had a hold on her.

She felt much better when Hypatia spoke, so she asked her a question, "What else have you learned from the Christian monks you saw at father's school?"

"I've learned more of Mary Magdalene and her writings. Did you know that she may have been the original author of the Gospel of John?"

Asclepe could not suppress her feelings. She gently cried, hiding her tears by turning from Hypatia. She wondered about Alexandria and the suspended tension in the streets over who ruled whom.

"Please be careful when we return to Alexandria, Hypatia!"

"I will dear Asclepe, I will."

Alexandria, Theon, and Pindarus

Alexandria was a melting pot of various types of people, some rich, many poor, and all keenly aware of the terrible power Cyril was gaining almost by the day. His sermons were not exhortations to follow Christ, but more like demands to listen to what his own ideas were. If his dictates were not obeyed, the rebel would soon find himself the victim of some horrible disaster. More often than not, resistance to Cyril's edicts would result in torture and death. And, no one was ever caught, though everyone knew the monks were behind it all. Peter the Reader, (the Jews called him Peter the illiterate,) was their leader, and followed Cyril's orders with gristly fervor, like a subjugated hyena. He was proud of his ignorance, and carried the Lord's cross before him in defense, demanding complete obeisance, rather, to his master's will and proclamations. Cyril was a master of strategy, emotionally, and by his words. He had named him, his favorite monk, 'Peter the Reader.'

Orestes, of all the citizens of the city of knowledge, had no fear. He was ever aware of the number of monks being recruited by Cyril, but they were still far less than his many well-trained soldiers. In a chess game, Orestes was king, and Cyril the bishop of Alexandria. There were many pawns for both of them to use, and many friends in Rome to help in the directions for their ultimate goals. So the game played on with few rules that didn't have a counterbalance. Orestes kept up the appearance of keeping the Goths away from Cyril, and so Cyril held back his attacks on the aristocrats, the Jews, and especially Hypatia and her father. Within his own 'realm,' Cyril waged unrelenting war against the Gnostics, and closely followed the beliefs of his uncle, Theophilus, whom he had succeeded. They were Nicene in their beliefs, a dominating sect of the growing 'Catholic' church, and they anathematized any belief not exactly their own. There was another element that was helping in the slow destruction of the Roman Empire. Many of the soldiers in its enormous army were becoming Christians, meek, passive, and horrified by their own acts of violence before conversion. The growing church was trying to take over the authority being vacated in the crumbling Roman dynasty of single rulers.

So it was that few really understood the impotency of the power of the empire. Philosophers, as students of history knew, and some of the top politicians in Rome knew, as they watched the empire vanish like sand castles into the sea, one by one. Gaul, Africa, Arabia; all the spokes were falling from the wheel, and now even the hub was waiting for the coup-de-grace.

But, little men saw little and feared not. For the moment, Orestes lived in comfort in Alexandria. But, Theon and others suspected that his strength would soon be tested. If there was sufficient success, Cyril would end the game quickly and be the sole heir of all Alexandria. The cursed library could then be destroyed totally, and the new order of Cyril would reign in aloof holiness. All pagan worship and knowledge would be wiped out, and the wolf would feel at home in the Lamb's clothing. Cyril would be known as the new 'Theophilus' in the triumph of Christianity over other religions.

·······

Theon found comfort in his studies, and so, for the time his daughter was safely away, he immersed himself in the ancient documents Hypatia had found and compiled. Theon had spent the entire morning locked away in Hypatia's study room. The old manuscripts had captured him and would not allow him to escape. They were like rewards for a child to the mathematician. He poured over them almost continually since his daughter and Asclepe had left for Athens. Even when he broke away to teach a class of mathematics, perform some inescapable function, or have a mid-day meal, as he now was, thoughts about the ancient writings never ceased. He was pondering the origins of Athena, whom the Greeks adored as well as the Egyptians who knew her as Neipthe.

When Pindarus spoke, he did not turn to look at him.

"Do you like your lunch, master?"

As usual Pindarus had prepared his masters meal, and, as usual, lately, Theon ate with little gusto. His mind was captured and entertained solely in thought about the ancient scrolls.

"What? Oh, I'm sorry Pindarus. Yes, everything is fine, fine."

Even as he spoke, Theon drifted away in abstract reflection. Pindarus recognized the now familiar far-away look on his face. He knew if he stopped to ask his master what he was eating he would have to stop eating and think about it. But, he remained respectfully quiet, and much to his surprise, Theon spoke again quickly.

"Do you recall our discussion yesterday afternoon?"

"Yes."

"Good. We must explore the teachings of Thoth in yet another aspect. As you know, the sacred halls of the Great Pyramid represented his home. In them were taught language and letters. They were, of course, lost in the Great Flood, and the world was without knowledge."

"You said, if I remember correctly, that he carried the Divine Flame."

"Yes. He was worshipped by all for revealing the knowledge of the pyramid. The Ancient Egyptian Empire was strong, and lasted for many thousands of years. But, it was only an echo of their antediluvian accomplishments. After the flood, all that remained were the sand dunes of the Sahara. The Great Sphinx alone withstood the Atlantean disaster. Hypatia found the key tablet to translating the others some months ago. They called Thoth the One Divine Flame as his successors were also known, though none achieved his greatness."

Pindarus was Theon's protégé now, his simple yet satisfying meals a certain path to his mentor. Mathematics concerned him the most, but Theon had only given Pindarus two equations to solve; contemplate or equate Pi, and estimate the size of the solar system. He was far closer to achieving an accurate approximation of the size of the solar system than to finding a rational answer to Pi.

Pindarus studied many things, including the subjects of any of Hypatia's lectures he could attend. But, Theon was his mentor, and though he didn't have to, he would rather focus on Theon and miss one of her famous orations. This new topic of Thoth contained a fresh life, an interesting history, and a fascination for Pindarus.

"Thoth dwelt in the Great Pyramid, and yet, to my knowledge, no one in recorded history has found a passage to its interior. How can we account for this discrepancy?

"Pythagorus studied in the temple halls, and later revered the tectactrys- a symbolic representation of its form. If we assume the many writings and stories are only myths, where can we go from there?"

Theon stopped talking and looked at his student. It was a museful look; a face of question suspended in contemplation. It was hard not to concentrate on Theon's magnetism and accomplishments as a teacher. Pindarus frowned. He would always be a student, unable to expand or comment on Theon's words. Always studying, but never creating. He respected Theon even more when he realized that his mentor, too, was a student. In fact, all they did lately was study. He looked back up at Theon.

He spoke matter-of-factly, "If you are through with your self-indulging, we will continue. Iamblichus indicated almost a hundred years ago that the Sphinx has a passageway that leads through a maze, and eventually to the Great Pyramid. I am sure that if we research further, we will find other reference. I know that Iamblichus described a bronze door located between the forelegs. Only the Divine Flame and the other Magi could open the gate. It was held fast to the profane by means of a secret spring."

Theon abruptly stopped and gazed out the window to the streets and buildings below. The afternoon sun had filled the air with yellow rays of sunshine. They were reflected and absorbed on the alabaster white sides of the two story buildings. He traced a line of cobblestone along the nearly empty street. Businesses displayed awnings of various colors all the way to the library and beyond. The piper was calling him, and he knew it. He knew he had to return to his studies of the scrolls. He had already learned more than he could tell; about

Atlantis, about the early post-flood times, and the facts about the Ancient Myths.

He *had* to walk to Hypatia's study room by the library. He talked as if in a trance. "Come Pindarus. We must learn more of our One Divine Flame!"

Theon and Pindarus turned for the stairs that led down past the kitchen to the street below. Before they could reach the ground floor, someone approached the door. Theon was ahead of Pindarus, and so saw the figure of Orestes through the lite above the door. Orestes did not see the look of disdain on Theon's face, nor did he feel his contempt for the Roman officer at his side. It was too late to turn around and escape their meeting. Theon continued to the foyer. He stepped aside to allow Pindarus to open the door and greet the Prefect.

"Yes sir?" His statement was flat and matter-of-fact. On other occasions lately, Pindarus had used similar address to Orestes, and the soldier-as-policeman didn't seem to mind. But, now a fire burned in Orestes from loneliness. All his soul ached for Hypatia, and his desire brought out the ugliness he thought no one could see.

His officer spoke sharply, "Stand aside boy!" As he pushed open the door and entered, the officer brought his right arm up as if to slap Pindarus with the back of his hand.

"Lucias, enough! We do not wish to disturb Master Theon unduly." A strange smile crossed his face. "When is your daughter returning, old Master?" He was tired of waiting for her. He thought she would marry him, but he was denied.

"Well!?"

Theon wanted to speak out, to express what he felt about Orestes, but in sobering contemplation, realized that in an instant many lives may be forfeit if he spoke so. In Orestes' present mood sarcasm or disrespect would be very dangerous. He had just seen that.

He was cautious with his words. "Hypatia returns soon so that she may take my chair at the Great Library. As Chief of Police, you will be formally notified. Arrangements must be made for her proper protection. On this regard we should speak now."

Orestes spoke gruffly, "Does someone wish her harm? I have already warned you Theon, if you drive her away from the protection I can give her...if I find out you oppose our union, I will take any step necessary to protect her. Do you understand me!?"

Orestes turned and walked out the door, his officer following behind him. It was the third time he visited in as many days. Theon had not seen him this angry before. He muttered half aside to Pindarus, "The man is detestable."

Orestes, governor of Egypt

There was a candle of Christianity that burned in the man Alexandrians called Prefect. He could be kind and fair, even benevolent to the poor, and generous. Orestes had a religious tolerance for all sects of Christians, Jews, and the Pagan philosophies. His one major fault was his familiarity with military brutality, and he was not afraid to use it. He had toiled for years to earn a position of relative importance and power, and would not give it up easily. His titles and duties included governing and policing Alexandria, the third major city of the empire, and keeping trade routes open. Orestes had the Roman authority to use whatever force necessary, and the soldiers to follow his orders. His one minor fault was that of many. Infatuation with Hypatia.

Taller than the average Alexandrian, the Roman prefect caused most to back away in his presence. He made his authority evident by the tassels, bronze medals, and obviously military clothing he wore. Not everyone respected his power, however. Cyril, for one, was always undermining and criticizing his relationship with Hypatia and the 'pagans,' along with the Jews and other friends he had in the government. For this reason Orestes never went anywhere without at least one guard. Loud banging on Cyril's church doors showed his sour mood.

"Open these doors at once!" Lucius commanded. At no answer, both pounded again.

Finally, the caretaker slowly opened the heavy church door. He recognized the governor, and said with respect, "Good afternoon, Governor Orestes. How may I help you? "

"I must see the Patriarch on official business."

"Yes sir! Please enter this holy church, and I will announce your presence to Cyril. May peace be in this place, and with you, in the Name of Jesus Christ."

Orestes and Lucius entered the darker, cooler building, and closed the massive door behind them. Its closing echoed through the quiet Caesareum church and resonated lastly in the altar chapel.

There were many small nooks and side alters as well as elevated platforms. Upon entering, the worshipper could light a candle in the first devotional station. Several large gold crosses that had been plundered from the Novations stood on pedestals to either side of the large main room. Cyril had expelled the Novations from their church because he thought their faith a deviation from orthodox Christian belief. *His* belief in their wrongness *allowed* him to confiscate all of their properties, and he wasn't shy about admitting doing so. Cyril's office and living quarters were in a separate building connected to the main church by a long stone corridor. The thick wood door opened into the church and the caretaker looked out and waved to Orestes.

"Cyril will see you now," he said in a whisper as they walked towards him. "He said he welcomes you in the Name of Jesus."

"We are not here on religious matters, this is an official visit in matters of city government."

"Yes, sir." He opened the door wider, stepped aside, and repeated, "Cyril will see you now."

Orestes walked briskly through the corridor with Lucius just a step behind. Candles lined the walls every six feet or so in small niches carved into the stone walls. It was enough light to show the way, though it didn't reveal much, if any, of the details elaborately carved into the stone walls. Cyril greeted them at the door to his office.

"Blessed be this day, governor Orestes, and every day you grace us with your presence."

Cyril's sarcasm was not lost on Orestes, and he quickly replied, "Blessed be *everyday* indeed."

He said it with authority to intimidate Cyril, but the moment was brief, "Come in Orestes. Join me in communion, and let us break bread. Have some fruit."

The Patriarch offered Orestes a wood bowl filled with dates, figs, and other fruits.

"I am not here to visit, socialize, or on religious matters. This is most serious and concerns the welfare of Alexandria. I will not allow any more conflict between the citizens of this city, whether Christian, Jew, or pagan."

"I have no conflict with anyone who believes in Jesus."

"The relics of your peace with fellow Christians adorn your church, and fill your coffers. If someone differs in their beliefs you stone them or run them out of town. You continually stir the flames between the Jews and Christians. You have encouraged the destruction of pagan temples, some of which the Emperor resents, as do I, not to mention the citizens. You cannot destroy all art and knowledge because you don't like it. As long as I am Governor I will not allow it. It must stop!"

"Dear governor, if you would but attend my sermons more often, you would see that you are wrong. I seek only to spread the word and power of our Lord to everyone. To show them the path to salvation sometimes requires strong measures. The pagans have little respect for Jesus, nor belief in His Glory, and those who call themselves artists and intellectuals are in effect snubbing their noses at the wisdom of the church. And Jesus," he quickly added.

"You are wrong, Cyril, and you must stop the violence. You have personally run nearly all the Jews from Alexandria and plundered their treasures simply because they enjoy the theater."

"The way the dancers perform in pagan frenzy is an abomination!"

"You are wrong! I have attended many of their performances and find them relaxing and good for the population. I have given them permission to continue, by my edict, and you will not harm any of them, before, during, or after their performances."

"You have tortured to death Hierax, a devout Christian in my congregation, and walked with Pagans and Jews. I know in my heart that you are striving to be a good Christian, kiss this holy book, this Bible, and prove your devotion to the Lord."

Cyril took a thick book from its stand nearby and held it out to the Prefect.

"I know my idea of devotion is Christian, but much different than yours, and it is loyal to the Emperor of Rome, not the church of Cyril."

The Patriarch was angry and turned away. "I know nothing of any violence," he said impatiently. "If you have some proof, some specific charge, some accusation you wish to make, take it to Rome. I know nothing. I will likewise write to the Emperor of your doings."

"I'm warning you, Cyril..."

"Do not threaten me in my church, you are on holy ground. This meeting is over, I must return to my prayers."

"There is one more matter that I will advise you of before you return to your *prayers*. Hypatia is to receive a chair in the Great Library, in fact, her father's chair when he steps down."

"I have no concern for her, as long as she does not blaspheme against the church."

"Do not make me return in anger by fomenting any further trouble."

Orestes walked to the door to leave, taking one last look back at Cyril, but he was still turned away. Orestes and Lucius both left, walking quickly through the corridor and into the church. Their steps were loud on the marble floors back to the main door. The caretaker opened it for them and bid them good day.

The Lecture and Miracle

Hypatia pulled the reigns back with tender authority and her two loyal horses simultaneously clomp-clomp clomp-clomped to a halt. A stable boy ran to meet the chariot and its driver. They knew each other well and exchanged warm greetings.

"Good morning, Perceus, what a nice day today. I see you are in good spirits, your happy smile is most contagious."

"Yea-yea-yes. Bea-bea-bea-beauty fu-full, li-like you-you."

The boy was fascinated with her natural beauty. His eyes followed her white robe's subtle contours with adolescent awe. She gave a knowing smile to Perceus as she spoke, "May I walk with you to the stables?"

The boy stammered back, "Yea-yea-yes, pe-pe-please."

They walked the cobblestone path past the entrance to the lecture room and on to the stables 100 feet beyond. The horses needed no cooling down walk, they weren't even sweaty. As they walked next to each other, both leading a horse by the bridal, Hypatia smiled. For weeks her lectures had mesmerized their audiences as she expounded upon ancient mystery knowledge. Many waited in the adjoining Western courtyard for those inside to reveal the contents of Hypatia's famous orations. All left her lectures in awe of her knowledge and the articulation of it. Hypatia had gone back in time through the Greek and Egyptian Mystery cults and their beliefs. But, no one had expected today's lecture topic. Not even Hypatia, until now.

During the short walk with Perceus, she realized the recent lectures were but a prelude to her discourse on Christianity. She felt the time had come to reveal the secret mysteries of Christianity that she had learned to her students. She thought deeply about the consequences. Even asked Orestes his opinion. Would Cyril seek revenge? Would he try to punish her or those whom she knew? Although Orestes assured her protection, she wondered about Theon's safety. Hypatia made many silent prayers for him. An advocate of Truth, she knew no fear. The light that was in her could remain inside no more.

They reached the stables, and Perceus took the reigns from Hypatia. Their eyes met, the sparkling compassion glowing and pulsing in her aura, the deed she was about to perform manifesting, as a daydream, in her mind. She took the reins back from him and gave the horses to a stable boy nearby.

"Take good care of my girls, Yussaf. Follow me, Perseus," she said softly.

Hypatia directed him to a side entrance to the building. It led down a narrow hall to the lecture room that she was to speak in. Hypatia held smaller lectures in her home. Of the two lecture rooms, this was the larger. It was filled with students, not a few learned philosophers from other countries.

Hypatia was tidying up Perceus's clothes and hair as though he was her child, and said a few motherly words to him. He waited by the door as she entered the lecture room. Conversations became silent as Hypatia gracefully walked to the simple wood podium. All eyes and attention were focused on her unequaled beauty and presence. She took one deep breath and then began.

"My dear brothers...we have spoken lately of the healing centers, of the ancient Atlanteans known as the children of the Law of One. It is known of their alchemy that it healed the spirit and the body. This power was given to the old dynasty Egyptian Priests, among them Imhotep and Hermes. Through the Pythagorian Initiation of the Great Pyramid, Greece was able to benefit of the healing powers from the ancient mysteries.

"A tenuous force between our spirit and body, we have spoken of our soul as being an ethereal substance, a link between matter and our very being. How soothing the harmonic scales of Pythagorus to the weak soul in need of nourishment. He also had effective poultices for the injured body, and the ill. But, a new era has come for the spirit.

"We have spoken recently of Jesus of Nazareth and His disciples, and many ears are listening to us, but not all will hear and understand. I feel that the current leaders of the Christian movement are almost making the true meaning of His words obscure. Has anyone a good thing to say about these events?"

A murmur filled the room, but quickly ceased. It was a little shocking to most of her students that she would so openly and obviously belittle Cyril. A small wave from her hand, like a magic wand, had dispelled both shock and the underlying dislike everyone felt towards the Patriarch. They were all awaiting her next words, fixed in conscious awareness, more than simply entranced, truly, students.

"Jesus has surely brought to our world a light that cannot be hidden nor extinguished, even by the likes of certain monks that pretend to know His ways. He has said, 'seek and you shall find, humbly ask, and it shall be given.' We need not follow the religious fanatics to understand the meaning of His words. We need only hear His words as they are. Yet, many would try to hide or alter those words to gather selfish glory or power. I would say to you, contemplate His words to know their real meaning.

"In the weeks ahead we will be studying many of the philosophical ideals and truths spoken by this Man. This Son of God, His ways and His words, and the lessons He gave by parable will be studied in detail. There are three levels of teaching, I should say, three levels of *knowledge* concerning Christianity. The first is for the neophyte, and can be found in the words of the Gospels as accepted by the ruling Church and State, and can be studied by all. Since Constantine, Rome has endeavored to formalize Christianity according to its leaders' wills. Therefore we have Matthew, Mark, Luke, and John, but other important Gospels have been ignored, hidden, destroyed, and even deemed heresy. These four Gospels will introduce

Christianity to the neophyte, but even in them is contained a secret teaching, unknown but to the Initiate, whose writings and knowledge are hidden, or worse, lost to the world. I have spent many months, even years trying to gather these documents for posterity, but I think dispersing this knowledge to all of you is most important this day. I will speak to you of the original Disciples and their written words. Thomas, Matthias, Mary Magdalene, Phillip, and others all had something to say to the followers of Jesus. There are other writings in both Aramaic and Greek that are being eradicated by the growing Church powers. Clement has said that Matthias and Plato shared the belief that 'to wonder at that which is present is the best preparation for the knowledge of what is beyond.' Our studies will take us through the Gospels to an understanding of the secret teachings, and eventually into the experience of Heaven on earth. This is what Jesus has brought to humanity.

"Clement has also spoken of the three levels of Christianity. There are secret writings that will bring the Initiate into the realm of pure Christianity where one experiences, as I have said, Heaven on earth. This third level cannot be written, but is rather learned and passed on to the Disciples of

Jesus through oral tradition. It reveals the most sacred knowledge and mysteries of the universe.

"And now I feel the time has come to demonstrate the power of His love."

All eyes followed Hypatia's attention to the door. She reached her hand toward Perceus and called him by name, "Come in here Perceus, please."

The youth entered, his brown hair looking a little less rustled than usual, his clothes a trifle neater. He walked slowly, his eyes fixed upon the object of his adoration. Perceus stopped by the podium, still looking at Hypatia.

She spoke caringly, lovingly, "You need not fear, Perceus, we are all your friends. See over there, it's Jamal, and there is Marcus, and Noradomus. You see them, don't you?"

Perceus timidly glanced in their direction and acknowledged each with a slight nod. His attention returned to Hypatia and he nodded twice again.

"We wish to...generate the cure of your stammer, Perceus, and help you speak without this impediment. Would you like us to do so?"

Perceus nodded.

Not a sound came from anyone, as if everyone stopped breathing.

"Be aware now of the Love that surrounds us and warms our souls. From the darkness a light is born that always lived. Through our love see it grow forever more. Students of Truth, listen for the power of the words of Jesus of Nazareth, the Essene and Good Shepherd of our world. Father, Our Father, give to Perceus again his normal voice that he may share with us your Son's words. In the light of Truth we give thanks and praise to His words and deeds."

The room was silent. A light, an aura engulfed Perceus as a rumbling noise appeared to come from the area around his neck. The etheric energy filled the room.

The effect was as if someone had simultaneously lifted each and every soul from their bodies. The lightness was euphoric, and as everyone sighed, a number of students, as well as Hypatia and Perceus began to smile.

"Thank you dear Father." Hypatia was ecstatic.

Everyone's attention was drawn to the young man standing in front of them. He was speaking to a student in the front row. No longer were his words interrupted by stammer. In fact, he spoke clearly, and carried in his voice the deeper tones of maturity beyond his years. As Perceus gave his thanks to God aloud, many silent prayers came from Hypatia and her students.

Although many asked questions of Perceus, he answered them all in thoughtful and gentle reply. He spoke in metaphor and by example, and impressed upon many the magnificence of the True, Eternal Life.

Hypatia ended her lecture with 'The Lord's Prayer,' that she had heard at Plutarch's. She promised her students that the next lecture would be about Jesus and His teachings.

Most of her students gathered around Perceus after lecture, though a few spoke briefly with Hypatia before joining the crowd. After everyone left the room, Hypatia leaned against the wall. She knew that word of Perceus would spread like wildfire, and she sensed a foreboding gloom on the horizon of the future. "Maybe now would be a good time to leave with father," she thought to herself. "Maybe now would be a good time to go," she whispered.

Cyril, the Patriarch of Alexandria.

Cyrillus was a native of Alexandria, his coarse and rough face a product of five hard years spent in mount Nitria in the desert. There he studied theology in monastic discipline. During this time, he was reproved by Isidore of Pelusium, his long-time venerated monitor, for being preoccupied with worldly thoughts and interests, even in his solitude. Cyril ignored the admonitions of his teachers and fellow monks, believing that his desire for power was the natural course to be taken against the many 'heretic' divisions of Christianity. The more authority Cyril gained, the more he could direct the war against non-orthodox sects of his faith as well as pagans. His power reached its summit in the year 412 A.D. when he was given the patriarchal chair of Alexandria. He succeeded his uncle Theophilus, and was no less fervent in his attacks on the Jews and anything he deemed pagan or heretic.

"You called for me, your holiness?"

Cyril had just turned from the alter where he had been rearranging some items of veneration recently confiscated from the main Jewish synagogue of Alexandria. When he saw Peter, his chief monk kneeling at the railing, he made the sign of the cross and motioned for him to rise.

"Why don't we retire into my office, Peter."

"Yes, your eminence."

As they walked, Cyril spoke in a low voice, "Do you know why I call you Peter, the Reader? It's because you are like a rock, and because you can read the mood of the people. You are my ears and voice, and the leader of my flock."

"I only wish to do what you would bid me do. You are my father and link to God."

"If only everyone in our church was as fervent in their goals as you..."

"What can I do, your holiness?"

Peter stepped ahead and opened the door to his office. Cyril made the sign of the cross and entered.

"Please come inside, Peter, there is much to discuss."

Cyril was dressed in a white alb, much like a Roman toga but of finer linen. An expensive vestment for the average, even well to do priest, but the Patriarch owned only the best of all things. A braided white wool cincture bound the alb tight around his waist. At mass, Cyril wore other vestments that now hung on a wall behind a large wood desk. Hanging on separate pegs were his stole, chasuble, and cope and veil. Many gold relics stolen and confiscated from the Jews and other non-orthodox churches were scattered around the room.

"I summoned you here for a specific reason, Peter. We must be ever vigilant in our dedication to the Lord. As you know, we have succeeded in ridding Alexandria of many pagan and heretic influences, but there is much work to do even so. Orestes, though he claims to follow the teachings of Christ, has allowed many heretics to remain in our city, even supporting the Jews. I'm afraid he has fallen under the spell of Hypatia, a pagan witch and harlot and teacher of evil doctrines."

"She has many followers."

"Yes. However, we have God on our side, and we will prevail. Her evil doings will not be protected by Orestes very much longer. I have many friends in Rome, and our church grows in strength daily. Soon our city will become the light of the world, and we will be rid of ignorance and corruption once and for all.

"However, I am in a position now where I can no longer lead our brothers in any violence against Hypatia or any other pagan philosopher or thinker in Alexandria. It is important that I am disassociated from local events to further our cause and beliefs in other cities.

"Do you understand?"

"Yes, your eminence."

"I will not be held responsible by Orestes for any acts of violence during Lent. It is a time for masses and prayers, and I will be very busy in this church." Cyril reached back and gently brushed his chasuble with the back of his hand.

"I will see what I can do," said Peter.

"Return to me when you are done, and I will proclaim your repentance to the Lord, for He forgives sins and will stand beside you if you act always in the name of the church, and Jesus," he added.

As Peter bowed, Cyril made the sign of the cross at his head. He turned and left the Patriarch, a zealous monk in search of a deed to please his master.

The Murder

"Master!"

Pindarus jumped to his teacher's side in time to clutch his arm, and help him to a chair. Theon had suddenly slumped in mid-sentence. Now he began to cry as if an unseen spirit was torturing him. He was in intense pain.

"Master, what's wrong?"

Pindarus began to worry as his soul too sensed something ominous- a shadow on everything. "Master, what is wrong that this spirit grips us so?"

"My child...my child..." Theon was unable to say anything else, tears and sobs convulsing his slack form.

Pindarus could not help his teacher, his mentor, the object of his undying love, now broken and helpless in sobbing confusion. Pindarus hurried down the narrow steps, steadying himself on the parallel rails along the walls of the staircase.

He walked out the kitchen door and through a short foyer, past his sandals, and into the cobbled street. The first few hard steps reminded him of his forgotten footwear, but he kept on walking. It was as if he needed the sobering pain. Time

117

swirled before him in storm-cloud patterns of grey and white charcoal shades. Each hard step he took jarred Pindarus one step closer to reality until a spark of reason convinced him that he had been thinking wildly, irrationally. An anxious fear drove him to take an unattended chariot left outside a spice shop. Strong scents of clove, nutmeg, and pungent saffron danced through Pindarus's senses of smell and taste.

He cracked the whip over the horse's head and drove the white mare and chariot towards the museum where Hypatia lectured. The streets were completely empty. As Pindarus neared the last turn to his destination, the crowd of people he suddenly encountered made his heart race in fear. Over fifty people, mostly students of Hypatia, were gathered in small agitated groups. Bits and pieces of sentences stood out-

"They've taken her..."

"Where is she?"

"What are they doing?"

Anxious questions spoken with an underscore of helpless anguish. A young man Pindarus thought to know as Jamal came bursting upon the crowd from behind the borrowed chariot. He stopped a dozen feet in front of its white horse.

Pindarus noticed a red mass at the back of his head. He was obviously hurt by his labored speech.

"I saw it...I tried to stop it..." Jamal winced and clenched his teeth. He set his jaw and continued at several peoples' urgings. "The monks pulled her from her chariot...demanded her to repent...she said not one word as they tore her clothes off and slapped her...tried to stop them...they beat me then left me as dead...someone hit me with a rock from behind...they're going to kill her...they were pulling out her hair!"

Jamal fell to his knees and put his face in his hands as he began to weep.

A tall olive-skinned man named Marcus shouted above the crowd, "Everyone to the church...quickly!"

By now the crowd had grown to nearly one hundred worried students and friends of Hypatia. As they hurried to Cyril's massive church, more people joined them. They were all looking for their teacher who, not an hour before had performed a miracle before their eyes. It was as though Hypatia had held for them the torch of enlightenment that they might see. And now that light was gone and only faint outlines and after-flash remained for her students to remember. When they came upon Hypatia's chariot, most stopped as though waiting for her to appear. Only Marcus, Jamal, and Pindarus ran to the riderless white chariot and horses. Something caught Jamal's eye. He clutched the nearest arm and pointed.

"Marcus!"

Marcus saw the torn swatch of garment he knew to be Hypatia's. It lay in the road beyond the chariot in the direction of the church. Pindarus ran to the scrap and picked it up. There was a red stain on one corner that could only be blood.

Marcus had already motioned for all to follow when Pindarus handed the scrap to him. Jamal sat on the chariot's platform, weak from loss of blood and the beating the monks gave him. Jamal looked up as Pindarus approached.

"Go my friend, help Marcus and the others against the monks."

"I am Jamal, but first I must ask you to go to Master Theon at his house. He may be in danger and besides, you need your wounds attended to. Take Hypatia's chariot- I will meet you there, I hope and pray, with the light of our lives. Yet, I feel only darkness, and fear that it will not be so. Theon knew, and now he'll need us."

"Who should I say sent me?"

"Pindarus is my name."

"Go then, Pindarus, and I will go to master Theon after a moment's rest."

Pindarus turned and ran after the church-bound students, scholars, and friends of Hypatia. Marcus had reached the church square in front of its massive building. The center of the cobblestone square, now known as Cyril's courtyard, served as an outdoor 'mass' area as well as the hub of several streets. The area was strangely quiet with no one about. Marcus walked boldly to the large gilded doors of Cyril's church and tried to open them. They would not move. He pounded on one and shouted-

"Open these doors!"

Someone pried a cobblestone loose and gave it to Marcus. Marcus hit the door again and again with the heavy stone. Finally, an old man appeared. It was the caretaker, a frail man with silver hair and clear, sharp, bright green eyes.

"Yes, yes, why do you pound so on the door of this holy place?"

"Where are they all, old man? Where have the monks taken Hypatia?"

"I do not know, sir. There is no one here now."

"Tell us where they have taken our beloved Hypatia, old man, or you will answer to Orestes and the law!"

"Yes, I have heard how he tortured and killed Hierax the teacher for sarcastic applause to his edict on dancing at the theater. I believe he was charged with fomenting discord among the Jews and Christians, tortured, and then put to death."

The old man did not fear the crowd, or for that matter Orestes very much. Cyril always protected and defended those of his following. Yet, a pure light poured from his eyes, and so, neither did he fear Cyril. In fact, the better he became acquainted with the loyal monks, such as Peter the Illiterate, the more he wanted to leave the church.

He opened wide the massive church door and proclaimed in a strong voice, "The monks be damned! There is no one here," and proceeded to exit the empty church.

Jamal held his head in his hands and tried to will away the constant intense pain of concussion. He rolled his head slowly in a circle and from side to side. He took a deep breath and, suddenly, dramatically, Hypatia's last lecture played before his mind. He would remember every word of it for the rest of his life, and he hoped, beyond. She had given a stable boy with a stutter the gift of eloquent speech. And though she had explained the accomplishment quickly, scientifically to him after lecture, Jamal could not think of Hypatia as a healer. To him she was no less than a beloved goddess. Tears welled in his eyes as he gathered the reins and stepped up on the chariot platform.

"Tch tch, let's go home."

The pair of white Arabian mares turned instinctively towards their home. As they walked, the echoes of their steps beat a mournful tattoo on the empty cobblestone streets.

Theon, Pindarus, & Sufa Escape

When Jamal reached Theon's two story home, his eyes closed as he grimaced at the searing pain at the back of his head. Unsteady long dark fingers gripped the edge of the chariot's front piece. He stepped down, but could go no further. He collapsed in the street before Theon's door, blood still oozing from his head wound.

It was an hour later when Pindarus returned to his master's home. Visibly shaken, an echo of his horrible experience was etched in the sad lines and ashen features of his face.

He ran to Jamal. "Oh no!"

He kneeled at his limp body aware that Jamal was no longer alive. He cried in silence, a trail of tears rolling from welled eyes down his cheeks.

"Must all good come to this?" He sobbed, half to himself, half to the unseen higher realms. As he turned his eyes to the peaceful blue skies and high feathery clouds, a new feeling entered his soul. It soothed and lifted him as a mother her child. Then, a voice, as if from the depths of an undulating sea beyond the clouds,

"Blessed are they who suffer for righteousness' sake, for theirs is the Kingdom of Heaven."

Pindarus was left standing beside Jamal, an aura of calm surrounding him and making him think of the living. After a few brief seconds another thought entered his mind.

"Theon!"

He swung the door open and raced to the top of the stairs taking two at a time.

"Master Theon!"

Theon was not there. Pindarus knew at once that if he was still alive, he would be at Hypatia's study room under the lecture hall. He hurried back down the stairs, sensing, somehow, that he would never return to his master's home. He put his sandals on at the door. After removing Jamal's body from the street, Pindarus took up the reins of Hypatia's chariot,

"Tch tch, let's go girls."

At his gentle pull, the white mares turned slowly to the left, the chariot following. Pindarus had to find Theon, and he knew he would be at Hypatia's study. He kept the mares at a methodic, contemplative walk. The clop-clop-clop echoed in the empty street off the whitewashed two story buildings, and rang through the sullen air. It created a melancholic mood. Pindarus looked to the reins in his hands. "Hypatia held these reins so few hours ago. The course of her life in her hands," he thought. "How could she be gone? What happened?"

He was again riding down the same cobblestone road to the lecture hall. His search for Hypatia had yielded less information than Jamal had given him. But, now a déjà vu passed slowly before his mind in a nightmare. His soul, floating above his mind, brought him to the astral world, the dream world of experience. Like an eagle soaring, keen eyes aware of single events before and during the murder.

"Her hands..."

The image of her hands appeared to his inner sight. First etheric, and only her hands. Then she was touching the throat of Perceus. The miracle played before his eyes. He saw the lecture hall, everyone's soul elevated by the awe of her demonstration, experiencing the Holy Ghost and the enlightenment of joy. Pindarus now experienced it. His body shivered in convulsive spasms as he saw with soul and spirit. He could not hold back tears in the double pain of joy and then sudden sorrow.

"So quickly she was taken…beat and tortured… No!"

Now the events of Hypatia's murder played out in grisly detail. Pindarus was not there then, but he was now. He watched in his mind's eye the ugly crowd. It was a wide-eyed nightmare.

One man pulled her from the chariot by the yellow shawl about her shoulders. She fell backwards to the ground. Others were picking up rocks and had clubs. Their faces were contorted and ugly. One short, balding man clad in a dark brown tunic barked orders to the others and pointed at Hypatia. Pindarus could hear their gross words…

"Repent witch! Admit your guilt pagan harlot! Denounce your gods!" and other more brutal words of twisted hate.

Hypatia stood amongst them unafraid. There was a calmness about her that drove Peter the Illiterate insane. The small man walked to her and slapped her. He pulled her head back and glowered in her face.

"Who is our God, woman?"

He released his hold so she could speak, but his dirty face remained close to hers. He moved back a little as Hypatia slowly tilted her head forward.

"Answer me," he shouted from two feet away.

She spoke softly, "I know not, for you have not shown Him to me."

Her words made him furious. "Pull out her hair," he shouted to the monks. "Beat her!"

Pindarus saw Jamal enter the scene. He tried to stop the crazed monks, but he was hit from behind and collapsed. The monks tore off her white robe and pulled at her hair. Long strands of black hair were ripped from her head as others slapped her or struck her with sticks or clubs. They dragged Hypatia's slumped form across the church courtyard. There they stoned her. Under Peter the Illiterate's orders, his solid gold cross shining in the sun, the monks took Hypatia's body to the beach and scraped the flesh from her bones with oyster shells, and then burned her remains in a bonfire.

Pindarus reeled in horror. He stopped the chariot and threw-up as he experienced the smell of burning human flesh and bones.

．．．．．．

They had left little evidence of their morbid crime. As the mob of friends of Hypatia pursued them, always one step behind, the monks went back to the church. Hypatia's followers finally returned to the church where the murderers hid, just out of reach. Their holy building was a fortress in which they could find refuge. And, Cyril gladly gave them sanctuary.

The experience was crushing to Pindarus. He had walked the streets with Hypatia's supporters, but he hadn't actually 'seen' what had happened. He hadn't 'experienced' the horrible murder until now. When he reached the lecture hall, Pindarus could not dismount the chariot. He stood on its platform in sobbing grief. The horses rocked uneasily. Pindarus drew a slow deep breath. Almost the moment his mind calmed, he saw a monk emerging from Hypatia's study room. He held many scrolls under his arms. As he approached, Pindarus jumped from the chariot, no longer paralyzed by sorrow.

"Where are you going?" There was a sense of purpose and determination in his voice. As he took the scrolls from the frightened monk and gently laid them in the chariot, anger welled within. He could contain himself no longer.

"You bastard!" he shouted as he struck the monk squarely on the jaw. He fell back in unconsciousness. Pindarus hurried down the steps beneath the lecture hall. As he turned through the narrow passages, worry over his master increased.

Would Theon too be found lying dead, perhaps in a pool of blood like Jamal? He entered Hypatia's chamber.

"Master! Are you alright?"

Theon was not wounded, visibly, but was more in a trance. He seemed distant, as if communing with another dimension. His vacant stare took in no objects. His blank mind expressed no thoughts. He was standing, motionless.

Pindarus returned to the street, but the monk had recovered and left. There was little noise, only an anxious muffled din from the church many blocks away. The smothered chatter rumbled nervously in the stones of the streets. A melancholy sadness swept over Pindarus like a heavy blanket. He cried in his hands as he looked towards the now stormy heavens. Grey clouds turning ever darker raced across the skies.

He raised his hands high and shouted, "Father of the gods, have mercy on us all."

He went back to Theon only to find that a new life had entered his master. He was standing by a shelf looking through some papers Hypatia had bound.

"Master?"

He turned to his student, "We must take what we can and go. Take all of Hypatia's papers...take them, and I will take the most ancient scrolls. We can wrap the clay tablets in the tapestries. Take them down from the walls, please."

Something quickened Pindarus into action. A pulse of new life in Theon? He hurried about his tasks, quickly taking the first tapestry down. On it was a depiction of a sheik stealing back his love from her kidnapper. They rode off together across the brightly tented desert, jet black Arabian in full stride, the excitement of the moment captured in its wild eyes. Pindarus glanced at Theon as he began placing the clay tablets in the tapestry. He noticed that Theon's hair had turned as white as the polished alabaster walls of the Great Library.

Pindarus and Theon wrapped and stacked the many scrolls, papers, tablets, and writings, and placed them in the middle of the floor. Pindarus left at Theon's direction and acquired a medium sized wagon. When he brought it back to the lecture hall, he found Theon and a young woman standing by the entrance door that led to the passageways and eventually to Hypatia's study. All of the documents were stacked on the walk next to them. Pindarus recognized the woman as

Sufa, a pupil of Hypatia's. They turned to watch him approach. He brought the wagon to a stop next to them and dismounted. Without speaking a word, the three loaded the precious cargo.

Twilight faded quickly behind the shadowy, cloudy skies. A small patch of turquoise and orange in the west was all the dark rolling clouds would allow. Theon, Pindarus, and Sufa rode away from Alexandria into the night. Only Theon knew their final destination.

For long hours the skies covered desert sands and weary travelers with gloomy storm clouds. Like a thick blanket, the air wrapped them in its folds. Eventually, the skies cleared. No one spoke.

Pindarus silently wondered where Theon was taking them for awhile, then entranced himself in the rhythmic shuffling of the horses march. The cart they pulled made a pair of long parallel lines extending into the infinite night.

Pindarus thought to himself, "I can not hear them now that the sky has become still and clear, I can only see every star as a grain of desert sand sparkling in the moonlight."

Hours passed. Sufa sat wrapped in emotion. She wondered to herself if she would ever stop crying. It seemed to her that tears were running down her cheeks for hours. In fact, they nearly had. It was a sad pain that brought on another round of tears. Her feelings swelled and ebbed like dunes over the desert on which they traveled. She existed, a drifter through a holy sorrow.

Theon was no longer Theon. His mind had split into two distinct personalities. It had to, there was no one in the outside world of his being that could console him enough. 'Theon' was his silent half, while his alter ego soothed him. Quiet words spoken in magical whispers brought endless streams of comfort to him. Theon lived his life through the egoless mirror of caring, and was drawn past Hypatia's death into the worlds of Eternity. He knew that someday he would rejoin her. He had begun his quest, a lonely wanderer in a dark spring night.

Aftermath

She knew He would be handsome. She had dreamed of Him a few times before she... a sudden shudder drew her attention back to the oasis ahead. Silk tents of various sizes, one purple, one soft green, and many with striped awnings surrounded a fountain of water. It spilled into a containment pond on which floated strange and beautiful birds. The date trees throughout the area provided enough shade for a dozen goats and many chickens to graze. The grass was rich and green and filled with life's energy.

She was between the palms, floating towards the green tent now, then shortly she was at its door. A stranger came out, pushing the tent flap to the side.

"I have been waiting for you, please come inside."

It was Jesus.

He held the flap as she entered. The interior of the tent was spacious. Larger, it seemed, than the huge indoor room at the Library of Alexandria. Hypatia was surprised to find Julio sitting in a lotus position near a low wood table.

He entered after her and spoke, "I believe you've met in Alexandria, did you not?"

Julio and Hypatia smiled at each other.

"Yes." Many thoughts suddenly crossed Hypatia's mind, a mind no longer encumbered by the physical boundaries of time and space. The material limitations of the senses were gone. In their place she found the *experience* of truth, the many ramifications and possibilities of existence obvious. The knowledge created a mood of Divine frivolity. Her spirit glowed.

"Before I ask you any questions, I would like to know you better."

He looked aside at Julio, smiling, then back at her glowing visage.

"You will know all secrets, precious spirit. Come walk and sit with me in the groves, and we will talk of Eternity."

With a romantic smile, the Hypatia in her chided, "I thought you would never ask."

Author's Apology & Sources

To list every source drawn from would not only be an impossibility, but a lack of credit for inspiration gained from basic knowledge and instinct experienced throughout my life. If we are a summary of what we experience, imitation is the highest form of flattery, yet I wish not to copy others, but to represent a small voice repeating in a different way that which I have learned to the best of my ability. Truth is often the progeny of Intuition. The subject I tried to address is no less complicated today than it was when it occurred. History is filled by contradictions and guesses at what really happened, and has almost as many theories and opinions about it as people who study it. In summary, before listing sources, I would like to apologize to those many not listed, and give them equal praise in absentia.

I would also ask forgiveness for certain errors and literary license in this story. For one, the Delphic oracle was, according to most scholars, in ruins from a devastating earthquake in 373A.D. The Temple of Apollo, built above a fissure and at the center of destruction, sat almost exactly at the crossing of earthquake faults running north and south and east and west. The frequency of divinations was curtailed more from this historic event than because of Christian monks' prejudices, although they were about the business of converting or destroying other pagan temples throughout Greece at this time.

Another glaring mistake for which I plead guilty is the absence of an accurate accounting of Theon's death in 405 A.D. I felt the historical fiction in keeping him alive for another decade more compelling in revealing the love Theon had for his daughter and her accomplishments and works. To these and any other facts or faults (unknown) that have been made fiction, I plead no contest.

*Hypatia summary
Hypatia of Alexandria 370 - 415
JOC//EFR @ April 1999
URL "http://www-history.mcs.st-andrews.ac.uk/Mathematicians/Hypatia.hotmail"
*Hypatia - Biography of Hypatia
Jone Johnson Lewis
@2006 About, Inc., A Part of The New York Times Company.
*Hypatia of Alexandria

Wikipedia, The Free Encyclopedia

*Elbert Hubbard, "Hypatia," in Little Journeys to the Homes of Great Teachers, v.23 #4, East Aurora, New York:

The Roycrofters, 1908 (375 p. 2v. ports. 21 cm)

*Damascius: The Life of Hypatia from the Suda

From Damascius's Life of Isadore, reproduced in the Suda

Translated by Jeremiah Reedy

Copyright 1993 by Phanes Press.

*The Life of Hypatia By Socrates Scholasticus,
 from his Ecclesiastical History

*The Life of Hypatia by John, Bishop of Nikiu, from his

Chronical 84.87-103.

*Hypatia and Her Mathematics by Michael A.B. Deakin,

The American Mathematical Monthly March 1994, vol. 101,

Number 3, pp.234-243.

*Eashoa Msheekhah, Jesus Christ

The Name of Jesus Christ

http://www.v-a.com/bible/jesus.html

*Religious Tolerance.org

The Resurrection of Jesus Christ

Beliefs by the Early Christian Church

Written by B.A.Robinson

*Christian Love Turns Cold

http://jtf27.tripod.com/ltc-2.html

*From "mailto:gmiller@netcom"

Good question...Did the early Church believe in Reincarnation?

*Nag Hammadi Library Alphabetical Index

The Gnostic Society Library

*The Gospel of Mary

From the Nag Hammadi Library, James L. Robinson

@Copyright Knowledge of Reality Magazine 1996-2005.

*The Gospel According to Mary Magdalene

The Gnostic Society Library

Gnostic Scriptures and Fragments

*Mary Magdalene: Author of the Fourth Gospel?

By Ramon K. Jusino, M.A. copyright 1998.

*Lives of Saints :: Baramhat 8 Coptic Orthodox Network

1. The Martyrdom of Saint Matthias, the Apostle

*David Ross. The Gospel of Matthias. Rice University.

*The Gospel of Thomas. Published by Messrs. Brill of Leiden.

*The Gnostic Society Library, The Nag Hammadi Library.

The Gospel of Thomas translated by Thomas O. Lambdin

*Early Christian Writings Gospel of Philip

English Translation by Wesley W. Isenberg

Early Christian Writings Copyright 2001 - 2006 Peter Kirby

*Early Christian Writings The Lost Sayings Gospel Q

Early Christian Writings Copyright 2001 - 2006 Peter Kirby

*Paul, Saint. The Columbia Encyclopedia, Sixth edition. 2001-05

Copyright 2001-05 Columbia University Press

*Books of the Bible: Acts

The Bible Tutor

*Gospel of Luke

Early Christian Writings Copyright @2001-2006 Peter Kirby

*Paul's Sermon on Mars' Hill (Areopagus, Hill of Ares)

 in Athens Greece

Padfield.com - The Church of Christ in Zion, Illinois

The Unknown God by David Padfield

Church of Christ, 2340 Lewis Ave.,

P.O. Box 95, Zion, Illinois 60099

*Christianity: Definition and Much More from Answers.com

Columbia University Press Encyclopedia

*The Early Church - The Roman Emperor Constantine

Constantine - First Christian Emperor of Rome (285-337 CE)

http://www.request.org.uk/main/history/romans/constantine.htm

*Constantine I: Definition and much more from Answers.com

*A Dictionary of Christian Biography and Literature to the end of the Sixth Century A.D., with an account of the Principle Sects and Heresies. By Henry Wace

*Theodosius I - Wikepedia, the free encyclopedia

*Theophilus of Alexandria: Information from Answers.com, Wikipedia

*Medieval Sourcebook: Nicene Creed from

The Seven Ecumenical Councils, ed. H. Percival, in the Library of Nicene and Post Nicene Fathers, 2nd. Series (New York: Charles Scribners, 1990), Vol. XIV, 3 author and maintainer Paul Halsall   "mailto: halsall@murray.fordham.edu"

*Cyril of Alexandria (c. 375-444) C. Burk, "Cyril of Alexandria," Philip Schaff, ed., A Religious Encyclopaedia or Dictionary of Biblical, Historical, Doctrinal, and Practical Theology, 3rd edn., Vol. I. Toronto, New York & London: Funk and Wagnalls Company, 1894. p. 594.

*Catholic Encyclopedia: The Church of Alexandria

Joseph M. Woods transcribed by Thomas J. Bress

The Catholic Encyclopedia Volume I

"mailto:Copyright@1907" by Robert Appleton Company

Online Edition Copyright @2003

By K. Knight

Nihil Obstat, March 1, 1907. Remy Lafort, S.T.D., Censor Imprimatur. +John Cardinal Farley, Archbishop of New York

*Christian Classics Ethereal Library

NPNF (V2-02), by Schaff, Philip

*Vestments of Catholic Priests and Bishops - Religion Facts

Catholic Priestly Vestments

Victor Schultze , "Vestments."

New Schaff-Herzog Encyclopedia of Religious Knowledge
(Baker Book House, 1950).
*The History and Use of Vestments in the Catholic Church
by Rev. John F. Sullivan, The Externals of the Catholic Church,
P.J. Kennedy & Sons (1918). Imprimatur + John Cardinal Farley, Archbishop of NY, March 27, 1918.
*The Symbolism of Vestments
Orthodox America   Reader Phillip Blyth
(From a talk given at the St. Herman Winter Pilgrimage,
Redding, California, 1983).
*Encyclopedia Coptica:
The Christian Coptic Orthodox Church of Egypt
*The Decline of the Library and Museum of Alexandria
By Ellen Brundige December 10, 1991
*The Scorpion in Ancient Egypt
The Ancient University of Alexandria (The Mouseion)
By Jimmy Dunn Copyright 1999 - 2005 by Intercity Oz, Inc.
*Goddess Worship

That real "old time religion?"

Copyright @1995 to 2005 by Ontario Consultants on Religious Tolerance Latest update 2005-DEC-10 Author B. A. Robinson

*Science and Technology at Scientific American. com:

Questioning the Delphic Oracle- -[Archeology]... @1996-2006 Scientific American, Inc.

*"The Delphic Oracle" by Eloise Hart (From Sunrise magazine, October/November 1985;

Copyright @ 1985 Theosophical University Press)

*Papyrus Reveals New Clues to Ancient World National Geographic News

National Geographic.com

@1995-2005 National Geographic Society

*"Apollo" created on 03 March 1997

Encyclopedia Mythica

@MCMXCV - MMVI Encyclopedia Mythica.

*Library 14 Appendix 2--The end of the Library The Ancient Library

<u>In Appreciation of consultation services:</u>
<u>Jspector@cfl.rr.com</u>

Thank you Cheri for all your hard work.

Cover design by Cheri Sweet-Jackson from: Gasparo's signed sketch of Hypatia used as an insert in Elbert Hubbard's pamphlet, Little Journey's into the Homes of Great Teachers, Vol. 23, No. 4, published in Oct. of 1908. (Information obtained via "Free Images from HYPATIA.ORG")

With special thanks to Authorhouse.

Printed in the United States
91102LV00001B/34-81/A